SOUNDS OF THUNDER

"Walk toward the sound of the guns."

Lewis Bowman looked to his right and to his left. None of the men, some of them as young as he was, had anything to say in response to the captain's order. What could they say? Even though the order made no sense—even a fifteen-year-old like him could see that—all of them were wearing the same uniform. Union blue. When you wore that uniform you did whatever the men with stripes on their shoulders said, especially when it meant you were about to march into a meat grinder.

This captain was a new one. He hadn't been in a battle yet and he looked like he was eager for it. Lewis wasn't quite sure what his name was. Either Sumber or Dumber. Probably the second one.

"Most of 'em," Artis had said, "is eager for it till they get the first bullet in 'em."

Their last captain had died right in front of Lewis' eyes in the second battle at that little farm where the Rebs were hiding behind the rocks, not walking out in broad daylight like cows being driven to the slaughter. That captain, Evans was his name, had raised his sword and started saying something. Lewis remembered every word.

"Boys of New York," Captain Evans had said, "let us show them what we are made of. . ."

Then the mortar shell that landed on his feet did a better job than his words of showing what he was made of—mostly blood.

Lewis looked behind him and caught a nod from Artis Cook. The same grim nod Artis had given him as they watched the men from the other company pour down the slope like ants streaming out of a hill some farmer kicked while plowing. Just like those ants, the men of that company had gotten stomped by the cannons and mortars and minnie balls.

If we be ants, Lewis thought, *them Rebs is hornets.*

That first assault was over quicker than a summer downpour,

thunder and all. All that was left was not pools of water in the sun but piles of dead and dying men, some crying out for their mothers with their last breaths.

The firing had stopped as soon as the last of the men in Union blue went down. The Rebs were short of ammunition, like always. They made up for it by making every cannon shot and mortar shell and ball of lead count.

Lewis kept his eyes locked on the eyes of Artis Cook. He'd not met Artis but two weeks ago, but they had formed a bond. Not only were they the same age, but their brown faces showed that the two boys had more in common than a life spent in the sun. They were both Indians.

Lewis remembered how they met. At the bivouac outside of Gettysburg he had smelled something cooking from back in the brush. He had looked around. No one else seemed to have caught the scent. Then he made as if to go and answer a call of nature. When no one was looking, he started to work his way back into the thick woods, moving so quiet that none of the other men in the company would have heard him. It was how he'd been taught to move by his father. Quiet as he was, the one who'd been cooking had heard him. When Lewis entered the little clearing, he saw the fire, the rabbit on the spit, but no sign of the one who had caught it. Lewis understood. He raised his hands over his head.

"You got me," he said in a soft voice. "Come on out, I'm a friend."

"Turn around," an equally soft voice answered.

Lewis turned to look into the gun barrel and then the smiling eyes of a young man with long jet-black hair covered by a Union cap, a face round as a circle, and a nose that looked to have been broken more than its share of times. Then Artis Cook lowered his gun.

"Let's eat," he had said.

From then on, wherever Lewis was, Artis was close behind. Artis had been separated from his own company—a good many of them Mohawk Indians like himself, volunteers from the St. Regis Reservation. In the last battle there had been such a scattering of men that new regiments and companies had to be put together like patchwork quilts from the sewn remnants of torn clothing. Artis had ended up assigned to Lewis' squad, a private like himself. The first time they spoke to each other had been that day over the rabbit, but the two young men had been silently watching each other ever since Artis' arrival.

Foot of the Mountain
and other stories

Foot of the Mountain
and other stories

joseph bruchac

Illustrations by Chris Charlebois

Holy Cow! Press • Duluth, Minnesota • 2005

Cover art and chapter heading images by Chris Charlebois
Author photograph by Mike Greenlar

We gratefully acknowledge Erik Sommer for his careful editorial attention to these stories.

 Design by Lisa McKhann (Duluth, Minnesota). Printed and bound in the United States of America.

ISBN-13: 978-0-930100-62-9; ISBN-10: 0-930100-62-X

Library of Congress Cataloging-in-Publication Data

Bruchac, Joseph, 1942-
Foot of the mountain and other stories / by Joseph Bruchac
p. cm.
ISBN 0-930100-62-X (alk. paper)
1. Abenaki Indians—Fiction. 2. Indians of North America—Fiction. I. Title.
PS3552.R794F66 2004
813'.54—dc22 2004043549

This project is supported, in part, by a grant from the Outagamie Charitable Foundation and by donations from generous individuals.

Holy Cow! Press books are distributed to the trade by Consortium Book Sales & Distribution (Saint Paul, Minnesota). For personal orders, catalogs, or other information, please write to:
Holy Cow! Press
Post Office Box 3170
Mount Royal Station
Duluth, Minnesota 55803

Visit our website: www.holycowpress.org

CONTENTS

PART ONE

Sounds of Thunder 9

Gifts 17

Bear Child 25

Mamakaden: Foot of the Mountain 31

A Panther in the Attic 43

Growing Season 53

Bone Girl 59

The Hungry One 63

Bad Meat 71

Bearskin Robe 75

Sojy Visits His Friends 79

PART TWO

Seeing the Circle: The Wisdom of Native Stories 83

The Truth of the Telling 91

At The End of Ridge Road: From a Nature Journal 95

For the Little People 111

The Snapping Turtle 117

Tickling a Trout 129

Hollyhocks 133

Acknowledgements 136

About the Author and Artist 137

Dedicated to the memory of Lee Francis,
who devoted so much of his heart and spirit
to the nurturing of other Native writers.

PART ONE

"You're Indian," Lewis said.

"Uh-huh."

"Mohawk, I'd bet," Lewis continued. It was already clear he'd have to carry most of the weight of words. It didn't make him uncomfortable. He was used to such conversations.

"Humh," Artis answered. "You?"

"Mostly," Lewis said. "We got some French and some of us call ourselves that, just to avoid trouble, you know? I was born up to St. Francis, but my family has been coming down to Saratoga for years. That's where I joined up."

"Abenaki?" Artis said, raising an eyebrow.

"That's right," Lewis said. "I be St. Francis Abenaki."

Artis laughed. "Then you should not of ate that rabbit." He slapped the trunk of the pine tree next to him. "You should have et this, you Adirondack!"

It was the longest statement yet, the most words Lewis would ever hear at one time from his new friend. But it made him angry. *Adirondack!* That was the word the Iroquois used for his people who sometimes used the inner bark of pines for food. *Adirondack* meant his people were porcupines, foolish bark eaters.

Lewis narrowed his eyes. "Well, you know where you got your name, don't you, Mohawk? We give it to you. *Maguak!* That means coward in my language."

Artis didn't answer with words. In one jump he was over the fire and the two of them were wrestling in the dirt. It ended with Artis sitting on top of Lewis' chest. One of Lewis' elbows had caught Artis in the nose and blood was dripping from it, but he paid no attention to it.

A rumble of thunder—real thunder, not distant cannon—came from the west. Artis nodded down at Lewis.

"Grandfathers, we call them," Lewis said from his back. A stick was poking into his shoulder blade.

"Uh-huh," Artis said. He stood, stretched out a hand, and helped Lewis to his feet. Then he reached down to a pouch hung from his side.

Some sort of medicine bag? Lewis thought.

Artis held the pouch up and shook it so that it made a rattling sound. "Marbles," he said. "Want to play?"

Lewis grinned. "For certain sure!" he said.

Men they might have been in battle, carrying rifles and bayonets, but they also were still boys. Lewis pulled out the gray handkerchief that held his own small store of clay marbles. They made a circle in the dry earth and played until the light began to fail and the call back to camp sounded. From then on, whenever there were a few hours of quiet, that was what they did. They played. Sometimes it was mumblety-peg with their pocket knives, but most often it was marbles. Whether by luck or skill, neither of them ever won all of the other's, though every marble changed hands a dozen times.

Artis proved a good friend in more ways than one. Though others might go to bed hungry, Artis was not one of them. Somehow he always managed to find food. If it wasn't a rabbit or a squirrel, it was berries or roots. It seemed to Lewis that if there was ever more than a moment's pause in the line of march Artis would have a fire started and be cooking. Whatever he cooked or gathered, half of it was always for Lewis.

Today there was no time for cooking. Men were waiting on the other side of that pasture to kill them. The field looked peaceful enough. Where it hadn't yet been trampled down by the feet of charging men, the grass was waving in the summer wind.

It is just right for cutting, Lewis thought. *But the only thing that will be mowed here today is men.*

Artis put his hand on Lewis's shoulder. "Listen," he whispered.

Lewis listened. Artis had heard it before him. A roll of thunder sounded off to the west. A storm was on its way, though it would, for certain sure, arrive after the storm of lead and fire.

"Grandfathers watch over you," Artis said. The way he said it made Lewis feel calm. He and Artis had talked about Thunder. *Heno* was what Mohawks called the thunder beings, the grandfathers. His own Abenaki people called them *Bedagiak.* The thunder beings were ancient grandfathers who cared for the people. When they struck the earth with their arrows of lightning they were trying to destroy bad things. Then they brought the rain to cleanse the earth.

A bugle sounded. The new captain stepped forward and raised his sword. There was the crumping sound of a mortar shell being fired from a Rebel battery. Both Artis and Lewis took a step backward. But the shell landed well in front of them. The captain pointed with his sword.

"That way, men," the captain said. "To the sound of the guns."

Then they were all moving, walking one foot after another. The thudding and thumping of the cannons and mortars was starting, not just from before but also from behind as their own artillerymen opened fire. There was fire and smoke in front of them. It made Lewis think of the hell that Father Andre up at Odanak had preached about. He didn't know if he was on his way to Father Andre's hell, but he was certain sure heading into this one on earth.

They were too far away to hit anyone with their rifles yet and they were still walking. Men fell around him as dirt and stones went spinning past his face. His cheeks were both wet. When he reached up to wipe them clean his hand came down all red. He didn't know if it was his own blood.

Someone pulled on his sleeve. He looked over. It was Artis. He had his mouth open and was shouting something. Lewis couldn't make it out. Then he realized that he was deaf, deaf from the cannon ball that had struck so close. Artis jerked his sleeve again and there was a popping in Lewis' ears. He could hear again.

"The hell with walking," Artis was yelling. "Run!"

They began to run. Not away from the battle but toward the enemy line. If they ran there might be less chance of getting shot. If they got close enough they could fire their guns with at least the chance of hitting something.

A gray shape like a ghost rose up out of the smoke, thrusting a bayonet at the end of a rifle. It tore the shoulder of Lewis' coat before Artis leaped in and knocked the Confederate soldier aside with his shoulder. The man fell down as they ran on.

They ran and ran. Lewis felt as if his lungs were on fire. Then he noticed that things were quieter. The fighting was behind him.

"Artis," Lewis said, "we got through."

No one answered. Lewis looked around. He was alone. Artis had disappeared. He looked ahead. There, through the smoke, he could make out something. A tree had fallen down, knocked over by a cannon blast. It was a place where he could take shelter and figure out what to do next. Lewis began to walk toward it, his breath gradually slowing. Sudden as a squirrel, someone in gray popped up from behind the tree and fired. The Rebel soldier was no more than ten paces away, but he missed. The minnie ball passed by Lewis' face with an angry sizzling sound. Lewis raised his own rifle to his shoulder to fire. He knew that he would not miss. Then he saw the frightened face of the person who'd shot at him. The Reb was a boy younger than him, so young he'd barely been able to lift the long old rifle. Lewis lowered his gun and raised a hand. He pushed it forward and nodded.

"Thank ye," the boy whispered. He turned and ran. Lewis watched him go. The boy's tattered gray uniform was so big for him that he'd rolled the legs of the pants up to his knees and the buttonless coat flapped on him like a scarecrow's shirt caught in the wind. Lewis shook his head as he stepped forward and placed his hand on the tree trunk. He was only fifteen, but he felt like he was a hundred years old.

All of a sudden, the whole world turned upside down. Everything got blacker than the darkest midnight and then even the blackness was gone.

Lewis tried to open his eyes. He couldn't. They were glued shut. He went to raise his right arm to wipe his face clean. The arm wouldn't move and for a moment he wondered if it was still there and not blown clean off. He tried again and he could feel his arm now. As he strained to move it, a wave of fiery pain swept over him and he lost consciousness. Perhaps it was only for a moment. Perhaps it was for a day. He had no way to tell.

When he came to, he heard a strange rasping sound. Someone was breathing near him, ragged painful breaths. He realized it was himself he was hearing. This time he didn't try to move the right arm that was pinned beneath him. Slowly, carefully, he attempted to flex the fingers on the left hand that he felt resting on his chest. They moved! A great wave of excitement swept over him. An inch at a time he walked his left hand up toward his face. Something was crusted over his eyes. He scraped away the mud that had dried there. Tears flowed, washing his eyes clean, and he could see. The tree he had been touching still lay there next to him. Its bark was torn now by the second cannon blast that had struck so close.

Lewis was half in a sitting position, and though he couldn't seem to get up, he could move his head. He looked down. One, two. His legs were both still there. They were not in one of those baskets of arms and legs outside the surgeons' tents. One of his boots had been knocked off. There were his toes. He tried to wiggle them. All five moved.

"Hurrah," he said in a weak voice. Whatever had been done to him, whatever damage he'd suffered was mostly inside of him and in his right arm. But he was so weak, so thirsty.

"I need help," he said in a voice he knew was too small to hear even if someone had been near. He tried to pull himself up with his left arm, but the pain from his right shoulder and arm drove through him like a bayonet, and he blacked out again.

When he woke again his throat was still dry. It was so dry that he felt as if he couldn't breathe.

"Grandfathers," he croaked.

A distant rumble sounded as if in answer. Then the thunder sounded again much closer. The next flash of lightning was no more than fifty yards away and it shook the earth. But Lewis was not afraid. He could hear the rain walking across the dry earth toward him. He leaned back his head and opened his mouth as the rain fell, a steady, heavy rain. It wet his face, washing away the mud and blood of battle, quenching his thirst.

"Bedagiak," Lewis Bowman whispered. "I thank you for my life."

He reached out his good left hand and tore a piece of the pale starchy inner bark from the pine tree next to him. As he placed it into his mouth, he thought for a moment about what Artis would say when he found him. Then he smiled and began to chew.

GIFTS

The land went backwards past her as Emma watched through the window. The spring was further along here. There were leaves the size of a squirrel's ear on the oak trees and people were already planting their crops in the fields. As she watched, the fields and the telephone poles close to the tracks seemed to be going backwards rather than the train going foward. She wished once again that she was going backwards herself, back towards the station at Syracuse where she had boarded this train which was taking her far away from home.

"You are going for the good of your people," the minister's wife had said, as she turned to look back at Emma sitting quietly in the back seat of the Model A Ford with her hands folded over her single black bag. The minister's wife had to shout to be heard over the sound of the engine. She held her broad-brimmed hat tightly on her head with one hand, gripping the seat with her other, as her husband drove them to the train station in his new automobile.

That had been a whole day ago. They had traveled a long way since then. Emma looked over at Mrs. Smith, sitting on the seat across from her, eyes seemingly closed in sleep.

But Mrs. Smith was not sleeping. She watched Emma through lidded eyes. She felt proud that she was accompanying Emma to the school, delivering her to her destiny. Emma was a fine young woman and Mrs. Smith had always enjoyed having Emma visit her home. Though the Indian girl seldom said anything, her manners were perfect and she had a bright, quick way about her. When she played her violin her fingers were like small birds fluttering across the strings. Mrs. Smith had never learned to play any instrument—she just didn't have the talent or the patience. But she could triumph in the achievements of a girl like Emma, a girl she believed she was influencing towards a better way. It was her duty, Mrs. Smith thought, to help a young child find her way, especially one from Onondaga where it seemed that the old-fashioned Indian ways were growing strong again. Those ways might have been good for the past, but not for this modern world of 1930. A young woman just entering the 6th grade couldn't travel alone all that distance. so she had volunteered to be the one to escort the child to school. It was fortunate that Mrs. Smith had relatives to visit in Virginia.

Emma closed her own eyes, remembering the words others had spoken to her.

"You have a special gift, young woman," the principal of the school on the reservation had said when he called her into his office to introduce her to the two serious people sitting there. There was a very pale white man in a stiff black suit and a white woman whose face was almost olive colored. She wore the shiniest button shoes Emma had ever seen. They had come with the information that Emma Johnson had indeed been chosen—because of her outstanding musical ability and her potential for leadership. She had been chosen from all the other young women in her school to go to the Hampton Institute, a special Indian School in Virginia.

"There you will learn the skills needed to be a leader among your people," said the woman with the olive-colored face. Emma noticed how strangely she spoke English, though the woman's voice had a kindness to it that made Emma feel as if she was really speaking to her and not speaking at her. She looked up into the woman's eyes. They were as dark as her own and Emma found herself wondering if this woman really was white.

"Maybe she is Indian, too," Emma thought. "Maybe she understands."

"There is a new world of opportunity for gifted people of color," the woman said. "In this new world women will not have to be second-class citizens anymore. A woman with an education can be a leader, even if she does have to make sacrifices. She may have to leave her people behind for a time, until she has learned enough to help bring them up to her own level."

Emma nodded, but she felt sad in her heart. This woman, whose face was as dark as her own, didn't really understand. Emma knew that education was a good thing. She loved the violin she was learning to play. The music of Mozart and Bach was as special and moving to her as the sounds of the birds singing their chorus at dawn. But she would not give up her love for those bird songs because she had learned this newer music. And she saw that this woman, with her belief in education, did not believe that the old Indian ways were also a form of education. When she spoke about women becoming leaders, she spoke as if it were a new thing for Indians. But Emma knew that Iroquois women always were leaders. She remembered how her grandmother had spoken to her only a few days before. They were working in the sap house, boiling down the sweet gift from the maple trees to make syrup. Nothing had yet been said about Emma being chosen to go to the government boarding school, but for some reason that was what her grandmother had chosen to talk about.

"Most outside people don't understand. When you travel you'll find this. But remember that we women are the ones who take care of the families, take care of the land," Grama Phoebe had said to her. Emma's grandmother was one of the Clan Mothers. Her full name, as it appeared in the birth records, was Phoebe Big Knife.

"We women are always at the center of things," Grama Phoebe continued. "That is why everyone inherits their clan from their mother. That is why we are the ones who chose the chiefs and can take them out of office if they don't behave. That is why we women got together a long time ago and decided that it was important for some of our young people to go outside of our communities and learn in the schools of the whites. We Iroquois would have to learn about the ways of these new people for our people to survive. In those first days we only sent our young men. Sometimes that was a mistake because the white ways were hard for them. Some of them never came back to us. Some came back and were confused. For a time they even changed the way we did things around here and we lost our traditional government. They brought in something they called Rules of Order." Grandma Phoebe had laughed. "But it took more than white people's orders to rule us Onondaga women. It took us a while, but we put things back the way they should be. We got our traditional government back. Some of our young people who we sent out, they came back and helped us to survive. You speak to He Who Makes Everyone Angry. He was one of them. Take him this tobacco and sit a while and he will tell you stories about the schools."

Emma did not go that day to see He Who Makes Everyone Angry.

But after meeting the two Indian Education people in the Principal's office, she walked across the valley towards the old chief's house. It was a warm March day and the snow was all gone from the field behind the school. Other boys and girls were getting ready to play Long Ball. They called to Emma to join them, but she continued on, crossing the road. She went past the longhouse and walked until she came to the stream and crossed the bridge. The old man's house was up in one of those folds in their valley. There the earth was still bent from that time long ago when the Holder Up of the Heavens shook the land to wipe out the evil stone giants who wanted to destroy all the human beings.

He Who Makes Everyone Angry was sitting on his front steps, a cane in his left hand.

"My Grama sent you some tobacco," Emma said, after greeting him in Onondaga.

The old man took the bundle of leaves in his right hand. "Ah," he said, in Onondaga, "this is good tobacco. See how green it is?" Then they sat for a while in silence. A red-capped woodpecker was working its way along the trunk of a dying elm tree near the old man's house.

"All those trees," He Who Makes Everyone Angry said, "they are dying from a disease that is carried by a beetle. That beetle was brought here from Europe. Now all our elm trees are being killed. No one will ever see a lodge like the ones our people used to make, all covered with the bark of our elm trees." He paused and tapped his cane on the steps. "When you go to that school, be sure to eat well and get rest. Keep your heart strong. You must do this because there is always sickness at those schools. Those white people do not know enough about medicine to cure our people when they get sick. I remember the big graveyard out behind the school buldings at Carlisle. Every year that graveyard got bigger."

The old man tapped his cane gently on the steps, its rhythm exactly that of the red-capped woodpecker in the tree above them.

The clacking of the train's wheels was like the rhythm of that woodpecker and the tapping of He Who Makes Everyone Angry's cane. Emma tapped her fingers on the black bag which she held in her lap. There was not much in that bag, for her parents and the elders knew how little she would be able to keep at the school. Her father and then her mother had each held her for a long time before she left their house. No one had said good-bye. There was no word for goodbye in Onondaga, and no one wanted to say anything in English. There would be plenty of English spoken where Emma was going.

At the school, they would want to separate her from her old ways of doing things. It was common practice for them to cut the long hair of the boys and place them in military uniforms so that they would look alike and think alike and be disconnected from their old customs. They would not be allowed to speak their own languages. He Who Makes Everyone Angry had told her about the time he and a Seneca boy were whipped until they bled because they were caught speaking to each other in Iroquois. Then they were locked in a special dark room in the basement for further punishment. Four other boys were locked in there with them. After the teachers left them there, the boys had begun to tell each other traditional stories.

"I spent a lot of time in that room," He Who Makes Everyone Angry had said. "Those stories we learned from each other were so good that it made the beatings seem worth it. They just didn't understand that there was plenty of room in our heads for more than one kind of thinking. Maybe it was because their own heads were too narrow."

Emma had laughed at that. The way he said it in the Onondaga language was so clear that it made her see the meanings even better than she would have in English.

"They do not understand the way we Iroquois do," he had said, "that we human beings always have a lot to teach each other. We have been learning things from their schools for more than one hundred years now. They have lots of good things to teach. But we have much still to give to them. This is what I think."

The train was pulling into a station. Mrs. Smith, the minister's wife, touched Emma's arm.

"Stay close to me, dear," Mrs. Smith said. "Hold tight to your bag. We are in the South, you know." She gestured and an elderly man in a uniform came over and picked up her own three heavy bags. His dark face and hands were as wrinkled as the bark of an elm tree. "Follow the porter, Emma."

The porter had a red cap on his head and Emma watched it bobbing through the crowded station. He was wearing steel taps on his shoes. Emma heard his feet clicking as he walked, the rhythm almost that of a song. Mrs. Smith didn't seem to notice, though. They walked for what seemed a long time. Then Mrs. Smith called to the porter to stop. "Wait here for us, boy," she said.

Emma wondered for a moment to whom Mrs. Smith was talking. There was no one but this elderly man and he was not a boy. In Onondaga Emma would have called him grandfather, but she knew he wouldn't be able to speak Iroquois.

Mrs. Smith handed the porter some change. "This is for you to take especially good care of our bags," she said. "Now wait here. We will be right back."

The elderly man in the gray uniform and the red cap nodded and smiled, but Emma could not see anything like a smile in his eyes.

"Come, dear," Mrs. Smith said, tugging at the sleeve of Emma's dress. Emma, still holding her black bag, followed her around the corner. Just past the large sign with the word "WOMEN" on it and a red arrow were two doors. One door said WHITE. The door itself was white and newly painted and and the word was printed in neat black letters. The other said COLORED and that door looked worn, the letters as gray as the old porter's uniform.

Mrs. Smith looked pointedly at the two doors and nodded. "Yes," she said, "this certainly is the South! Now stay close to me, dear."

They went through the door marked WHITE. No one bothered them and no one seemed to pay any attention when they came out, but as they walked back towards the porter, Emma wondered which door she would have gone through had she been alone in this Virginia train station.

The old man picked up the bags as if he hardly noticed their weight. Mrs. Smith led the way, the porter and Emma a few steps behind. The porter looked into Emma's eyes and it was as if, for just a brief moment, he was listening to her thoughts.

"Long way from your people, child?"

Emma nodded.

"You just got to carry your home with you wherever you go," he said.

"I'll remember," Emma said.

"I bet you will." The old man laughed and it was a deep laugh that made her think of the sound of the spring flood waters in the stream at Onondaga. They were outside the station now and Mrs. Smith was gesturing to a cab. It stopped and she supervised the loading of her luggage before handing the porter a one dollar bill.

"Come along, dear," she said, already halfway into the cab.

But Emma stood there by the curb, looking up at the porter. She opened the black bag and took out the corn husk doll which she had brought with her from Onondaga. It wore a calico dress and had been made as corn husk dolls had always been made—made to remind the people of all the great gifts given to them. Those great gifts were the ones which can never be purchased, but only given freely—air and the water and the earth which nurtured the corn and the beans and the squash. But the gifts were also the gifts of faithfulness, friendship and understanding.

"Grandfather," she said, "thank you for what you've given me." Then she handed the old man her gift.

BEAR CHILD

Once upon a time, not long ago, there was a boy named R.T. He lived in the city with his mother and his father and they loved him very much.

People around them thought that his father was only a part-time bank guard, but he was actually an African prince. His father's voice was deep and kind. When his father smiled at him, it was like the sun coming out from behind a cloud.

People thought that his mother was just a temp, but she was really an Indian princess. She was as graceful as a deer and she taught R.T. words that no one else knew except for them. Magic words.

Their apartment might have been small, but it was really a castle for the three of them. Some day, when their ship came in, their castle would become huge and they would have everything they had ever wanted.

That was how his mother told him the story. It was a good story and R.T. would repeat it to his friends, especially Wasos, the Bear. But his mother stopped telling that story after the dark day in March when his father did not come home.

After the phone call, she had taken him by the shoulders and looked into his face for a long time. Her face was wet and her eyes looked so big.

"They shot him, Arthur. What are we going to do?"

He heard what she said, but her words were like a story he didn't believe. No one ever shot a prince in any story.

The days after that were so confusing. There wasn't much food in the little fridge. The apartment got cold. His mother wouldn't get out of bed. She wanted to sleep and sleep, like a bear in the winter. Sometimes she cried and said things that made R.T. afraid.

"They are going to take you away from me," she said. "You are all that I have left."

She never told him stories any more. R.T. stopped going to school.

He took money from her purse and bought food. His mother didn't ask where the food came from. She just ate it and then went back to bed. Soon all the money was gone.

R.T. was small. He wore his big jacket. At the store he put the boxes of food into his jacket. He could run fast and if they saw him sneaking out, they couldn't catch him. He brought the food home and made his mother eat. The television was gone now, so he sat and told stories to Wasos. They kept warm under the blankets, even though there was frost on the windows. Then it was spring. He and Wasos were warmer. But his mother was thinner. She looked sick.

One day, when he came home, people were waiting. He dropped the milk cartons and tried to run, but they caught him. He fought like a bear and growled, but they held onto him.

"Your mother needs treatment," said a man whose face was almost as dark as his father's had been. R.T. didn't listen. He knew the man was not a prince. He was only a social worker. He was one of them, the ones his mother had feared. The ones who would take him away.

"You have family," they told him.

This was not what his mother had told him. She had told him that there were only three people in their kingdom. Nevertheless, to his other family he was taken.

When he and his escort got off the bus there were trees everywhere. A man and a woman stood there. They were very old, R.T. thought. They were as old as his teachers at the school had been.

The woman smiled. "Are you our nephew, Arthur?"

He shook his head. "R.T.," he said.

The man knelt down and looked at R.T.'s bear. "Wasos," the man said.

R.T. was shocked.

"How did you know his name?"

"That's our old name for the dark brother," the man said. "I'm your Uncle Leon. Aunt Rose and I will take care of you for awhile."

Aunt Rose held out her hand. When R.T. just held tighter to his bear, she put her hand on his shoulder.

"Let's get you home and get you fed," she said. "We've got the whole summer to get to know each other."

R.T. was still bothered by all the trees, but he liked their house.

They gave him a room so big he couldn't believe it was for only one person.

"Marie, your mother, she used to stay in this room when she visited us," Aunt Rose said. "I'll leave the nightlight on."

R.T. hugged Wasos to his chest. The night outside the window didn't sound like the city. It was too quiet. There was a radio on the table by the bed. He turned it on so that things wouldn't be so quiet. Then he could sleep.

As the days went on, he helped Uncle Leon do things, like piling up wood and weeding in the garden. Uncle Leon gave him a dollar every day for the work he did to help them out.

"I don't know how we made out without you, R.T." Uncle Leon said.

When they were done with work, Uncle Leon took him for walks into the woods. R.T. would not take his hand, but he stayed close by his uncle's side. Before long, R.T. was no longer bothered by all the trees. Uncle Leon showed him how to find his way along the trails. There were no street signs, but he could look up at the sun in the sky or see the circled branches and marks his uncle had made on the trees.

"There are the tracks of Mategwas, the Rabbit," Uncle Lcon said. R.T. saw them.

Uncle Leon told him how things were done in the old days. One day he took out a small bow.

"It is time to learn how to make a fire," he said. He showed R.T. how to hold the bow so that it would make the spindle turn. R.T. tried and tried. It was hard, but he made smoke.

At night, Aunt Marie would tell him stories. Her stories were different. They were not about princes and princesses. They were about animals. The stories about Azban, the Raccoon made him laugh. He hadn't laughed in a long time. He wasn't sure that he was supposed to laugh.

Aunt Marie told him about the bears. Aunt Marie was afraid of bears. She explained how a mother bear defends its cubs.

"Never get between a mother and her cubs. Just last year a foolish man was killed near here when he did that."

Then she smiled at R.T. and pulled him into her lap. He didn't resist.

"The bears like to adopt our children," she told him. "Once there was a boy who was berry-picking with his parents. But he wandered away from them. A mother bear saw him and took him home. He became a Bear Child. He never returned to the village. That happened in the time of my own great-grandmother. Our people looked and looked for him, but he never came home."

She hugged R.T. hard when she finished that story. He no longer tried to squirm away when she hugged him. He felt warm and happy, but he also was confused. He missed his mother. How could she be happy without him? He got angry at himself for being happy.

He knew the name of the place where they kept his mother. He was able to read it on the letters that came to his aunt and uncle. One day he copied the address onto a piece of paper, printing it very clearly. He had enough dollars saved to buy a bus ticket to the city.

He knew that Aunt Marie and Uncle Leon would stop him. He felt badly because he knew that they relied on him now. They didn't know how they had been able to manage without him. But his mother needed him.

R.T. knew what he had to do. He would cut through the woods and go over the hill through the old field where there were berry bushes. Then he would reach the road where the bus stopped. He would use his dollars to buy a ticket.

He lay in bed that night holding onto Wasos. After it was quiet, he got up and put his clothes on. He put the dollars and the paper with the address on it into his pocket. Then he got back on the bed to wait just a little bit, but he fell asleep. When he woke it was almost morning. He slipped outside and took the trail into the woods. He didn't think that anyone had seen him.

The birds started singing as he climbed the hill. The sun wasn't up yet. The berry bushes were thick and higher than his head. It was like going through a tunnel.

As R.T. stepped out into the clear space on the hilltop the sun was just coming up. He saw something in front of him. It was like a big round stone. Then it moved. It lifted up a head and looked at him. It was a baby bear. Then another one stood up behind it. They were so close he could have reached out to touch them. R.T. didn't move. His heart was pounding and he held Wasos tight to his chest.

Then he heard a cough. It was so loud that he felt it vibrate through him. He slowly turned his head to look. There she was, standing like a person. She towered over him, her mouth open and her white teeth shining, caught by the light of dawn. R.T. knew it was the mother bear.

She looked angry. He was right between her and her cubs.

Then he heard a voice. Someone was singing a song. He didn't know the words, but they sounded so familiar, so magical. Like the words his mother used to teach him.

Yah weh do, yah weh, yah wey
Yah hey ya hey
Yah weh dah, yah wey, yaw wey
Yah hey hey yay

The mother bear turned toward the singing. As she moved, R.T. could see the one who sang. It wasn't his mother. It was his Aunt Rose. Even though she was afraid of bears, she stepped closer. Then she spoke to the bear.

"Dark sister," Aunt Rose said, "take pity on my little boy. Do not take him away. He is young and did not mean to trouble you. We love him and we do not want to lose him. Soon his mother will return to be with him. Take pity on us all."

The mother bear seemed to listen as Aunt Rose spoke. She dropped back down to all fours and swung her head back and forth as she looked at Aunt Rose. It was, R.T. thought, as if the bear was saying hello.

Then the mother bear turned. She brushed past R.T., so close that he felt the warmth of the her breath. She cuffed one of her cubs with a paw and shoved the other one with her head so hard that it rolled over. R.T. felt a smile coming over his face as he watched the bears disappear into the berry bushes. Then Aunt Rose was next to him.

"R.T.," she said.

Aunt Rose's voice was warm and he realized how much it was like his mother's voice. One day his mother would be here, too. He knew that as surely as he knew that the mother bear would always defend her little ones. The happiness he felt in his heart was no longer confused. It wasn't once upon a time. It was now.

"Let's go home," he said.

MAMAKADEN: FOOT OF THE MOUNTAIN

Bigman looked down into the valley. It was quiet down there, aside from the small curl of smoke that rose, almost like the feather of a gray goose, from the small shelter made out of wood at the valley's far end.

Quiet. It was too quiet. He shook his head. The hunters that came just before the snow had driven away the deer. They were not good hunters. They didn't live here like the old woman. They just came every year. They made so much noise that the bigger game animals simply left the valley. It was as if those people didn't know how to hunt. Or perhaps they didn't really come to hunt. Perhaps they just came to shout at each other and become lost in the forest. Now and then one of them would become so lost that no one would ever find him again. Well, almost no one. Bigman rubbed his chin with one long finger.

He could have followed the deer out of the valley. That was what his mother and his sister had done. But he was stubborn. He was not ready to leave yet. He would stay here even if the hunting was not that good. His mother and his sister looked at him before they left. He turned away from them and pretended to be watching the sunset. Part of the reason he decided to stay was that they wanted him to leave. That was his stubbornness. Besides, he had grown used to watching the old woman. He was not yet done watching her.

There was, of course, another reason for his staying. It was the reason he refused to consider. It was his feet. They were sore and one of them was swollen. It would have been hard for him to walk as far as his mother and his sister planned to walk. Perhaps he could not have even kept up with them. That would have made him ashamed and he did not want to feel shame. So he simply watched the sunset as he heard them move away quietly. It was a good sunset. There was red in it that was quite close to the color of the blood that comes from the mouth of a deer as it lies dying on the snow. There was yellow that was even brighter than the leaves of the chattering trees just before they fall to the ground. There was pink much like that on the chest feathers of the little birds that sometimes flew down and landed on the branches next to him while he was sitting on his favorite stone and watching the valley. There were also other colors that he had seen only in sunsets. A fine sunset indeed.

At last, the sunset was swallowed by the darkness. That was when he turned around to see that he was, indeed, alone.

The aloneness did not bother him at first. But as the sun rose and then set, rose and set again, the being all alone rose in him and did not set. So he began to go further down into the valley, closer to the old woman's cabin. He went close enough to hear her voice as she sang to herself. Perhaps that was why she did not seem to feel alone. She sang to herself.

Bigman knew he was not a good singer. So he did not even try. Instead, he began to sit outside, close to the hole in the wall of her shelter, to hear her songs at night. She sang in the old language. There was a time when all of the people who came into the valley used that language. Now he hardly ever heard it. It was much gentler than the language used by the hunters. It lacked the anger and confusion that he always heard sooner or later in their words. Also, none of those hunters ever sang. Perhaps that was why there was so much anger and confusion in them. Maybe they made so much noise because they couldn't sing.

Bigman hummed very softly as the old woman sang, just loud enough so that she could not hear.

The sun rose and set, rose and set again. He was digging roots with a sharp stick on the steepest slope. He stepped and his foot slipped on the snowy earth. His other foot could not hold him. His feet! He remembered being angry at his feet as he fell, snow flying up in a cloud above his face as he rolled. . . and then the sunset came very early and very fast in a sudden burst of colors followed by a very dark night.

When he woke up at the bottom of the slope the morning had come. He wiped the snow from his face and opened his eyes. The world looked very strange. Then he realized he was upside down. He could see upslope where he had fallen. Limbs had been broken from the trees as he rolled and slid. One of his legs was caught between his body and the broken limb of a tree. Stones had also come down with him as he fell. Two of them held him in place, pinning one arm beneath him. He tried to move them with his free arm, but the stones were even more stubborn than him. He was certain that only his foot was hurt, that he would be able to move his other arm if he could free it. But he could not. He was caught.

He moaned. That did not help. He sighed. That, too, did not satisfy him. So he tried humming. That was better. He closed his eyes and kept on humming. He hummed the song the old woman had been singing and he thought of her. He hummed it until his throat began to hurt from the dryness. Then he opened his eyes to see if it had worked.

It had. The old woman was standing there. He smiled at her.

Micigan gwina! You're a big one.

He smiled at her, being careful not to show his teeth so that she would know his smile was a friendly one, even if it was upside down. The old woman stepped a little closer and held out her hand. He reached out his free arm and gently touched her hand with one long finger, stroking the back of her hand. It was important not to frighten her. He knew how easy it was to frighten people when they did not know you.

Well, she said.

He tapped one finger against his dry lips.

The old woman sighed. Having decided, she stepped even closer and untied the container from her side, opened it and poured water into his mouth as he lifted his head.

The water was very good. Not being caught would be better. Bigman tapped her gently on one of her shoulders and placed his hand on the stone that was trapping him. If it was moved, he would be able to work himself free. Then he pointed at a thick fallen branch that was the thickness of his wrist and as long as the old woman was tall. He made further motions with his free hand. If that branch was wedged in the right place, a place Bigman couldn't reach himself, the stone could be pried free.

Wawodamnwinno. You're a smart one now, aren't you?

The old woman picked up the branch with both hands. She was stronger than Bigman had expected. She climbed up onto the pile of stones and earth, wedged the stick in and began to press her weight down on it. Slowly, the stone moved. Bigman groaned with the effort as he slid his trapped arm out. Though his arm and hand felt bruised, his skin was tough. There was almost no bleeding. Nothing was broken.

The old woman dropped the stick and placed her hands on the knee of his trapped leg. Bigman motioned for her to climb down and move back. Again, proving her intelligence, she did as he wanted.

The thick muscles in his stomach tensed like the knotted roots of trees as he sat up, twisted his body, and shoved with his free leg. The branch that had trapped him cracked and then broke loose from the pile of snow and earth and stones. He was free.

Bigman slid down the slope and sat on the ground. He rubbed his leg and his foot with both hands, bringing the feeling back into them. Something touched his shoulder. It was the old woman's hand. She had not run away. This pleased him. He had roared loudly when thrusting against the stick to break himself free, but it had not frightened her. She was both intelligent and brave.

Let me see that.

Her hands were on his foot now. The one which had been sore for a long time. The one which had betrayed him into falling.

Ahhh.

She stepped back and motioned up with both of her hands.

Bigman stood. Her head only came up to his waist as he looked down on her. She stepped back and motioned to him again with her hands.

Baji. Come here, you.

Bigman walked toward her. He tried not to limp.

Unh-hunh.

The old woman looked at his feet, then pursed her lips. She rubbed her hands together, then nodded as if coming to a decision. With one hand she reached to Bigman. Bigman lifted his own hand toward her. Her hand was just large enough for her to wrap it around his pointing finger.

Baji.

Then she turned, pulling him after her.

When they reached her shelter the old woman placed her hand on the fallen trunk of a tree near the edge of the small clearing.

Oskidabi biyo. Sit you down on this log.

Bigman placed his hands on the log and sat down, thrusting his legs out in front of him. He sighed. It felt good to take the weight off his sore feet.

The old woman went into the shelter. Bigman heard the sound of things being moved around. Then he heard the sound of something being dropped.

Dammit. *Dodaka?* Where the hell? If you little ones have been hiding my kit on me again I'm not leaving no more food out for you. *Debestamasi?* You hear me? All right! *Wliwini.* Thank you.

The old woman came out carrying a bag that she thumped down onto the ground next to his feet. As she bent down, reaching inside it for something, she began to sing softly. It was a song that Bigman had not heard before. It was a good song. He began to hum along with her. She stopped singing and looked at him.

So it's you I've been hearing at nights.

Bigman looked at her face. She didn't seem angry at him. He smiled.

Giawaldam? You lonesome?

She pulled a hard bottle from the bag. Bigman had often seen bottles like it before. The hunters left such hard bottles in the forest. They were better than the soft bottles which looked hard but were as easy to crush in your hands as the dried shell left behind by a little crawling one. It was interesting to hold such a hard bottle up and look through it at the sun. He kept many of these hard bottles that he had collected in a cave further up the mountain. She pulled a piece of wood from the mouth of the bottle and smelled it.

Gatata. Good and ready.

She tipped the bottle and poured the dark water in it onto a cloth. Then she began to clean Bigman's swollen foot. It was strange how the dark water felt cool at first and then seemed to grow hot.

Akwitta modkawa. Sit still now!

Bigman did his best to stop squirming. The dark water had grown so hot that it felt as if it was burning him. But the old woman was singing now. That made it easier. He began humming along again.

Later in the day the old woman made a fire. She set up a pot and cooked food. It tasted good. As he ate, the old woman seemed very happy, especially when he cleaned all that was left out of the pot with his fingers. When he was done, his stomach made a growling sound. Bigman limped off into the bushes, noticing that his swollen foot no longer hurt as much as before. When he was done, he came back to the fire. The old woman was still sitting there. This time when she began to sing it was one of the songs Bigman had heard before. He hummed along until he fell asleep.

The next morning, when he woke up, the old woman was gone. He thought of going to look for her, but decided that would not be the right thing to do. Instead, he just waited. Sure enough, before the sun was a hand's width above the mountain, she came back. This time she carried a smooth thick piece of animal skin with her. There was no hair on it, but it still had the smell of the moose, even though it also had the strong sweet scent of smoke to it. She carried other things as well.

Bigman raised a hand toward her, one long finger held up in greeting.

Dalskawobo. So he sits and waits. Guess I'm stuck with you.

She knelt down by his feet and held the moose skin up against the bottom of his foot. She made marks on the skin with a stick that left lines behind it. Then she began to work. Bigman watched her. He liked watching people do their work, but he had always watched before from a hiding place. Never from so close. The sun moved as the old woman worked. When the sun was at the top of the sky, the old woman stopped working and took dried meat from a bag. Fish meat. Good tasting. She ate one piece. Bigman ate the rest.

By the time the sun was at the edge of the sky she was done.

Nasto. Put it on.

She worked over one foot and then the other, pulling, pushing, tying. Finally it was on. Bigman stood up and took a few steps. The earth that had felt so painful to his feet no longer touched them.

The sun rose and set, rose and set. A few nights later a deer that had come back in the valley walked along the trail where Bigman was waiting.

When the next sun rose and the old woman came out of her shelter, the deer hung from a tree limb.

Wliwini, Mamakaden. Thank you, Foot of the Mountain.

Where he was hidden further up the slope, Bigman heard the old woman's words and smiled.

The sun rose and set again. The growling sound Bigman had heard before came from the far mouth of the valley and then stopped. Usually he heard such a sound before the hunters came walking in, but this was not the time for the hunters to come. Bigman watched. A lone man finally appeared on the trail. Bigman followed quietly. The lone man was a good walker, pretty quiet, and he seemed to be seeing things with his eyes. He went straight to the shelter where the old woman lived.

Auntie.

My nephew.

Bigman was relieved when the old woman ran to the lone man and embraced him, but he did not come out. He stayed hidden. The two people talked to each other.

You ready to come home now, Auntie?

No.

Aren't you lonely here, Auntie?

The old woman sat down on the log where Bigman usually sat. She looked up the slope, right toward the place where Bigman was hiding and a small smile came onto her face.

No.

The young man sat down next to her.

Listen. You can't fight them.

I can't?

No. When they did the survey they decided this land had been left out of the park. So now they can come into it and survey it for mining. They can take their dozers and open up a temporary road into the valley. This place is open for mineral exploration until they can get something through the legislature to redraw the lines. But that will take months and by then it'll be too late. This valley isn't protected now.

The old woman looked up again at the bushes where Bigman was hiding. Her smile got broader.

Oh, is it not?

The young man placed one hand on the old woman's shoulder.

Auntie, I know you believe the ancestors watch over this valley. Remember, you told me all those stories. I know that it was our land way back then.

Still is.

The young man looked up at the sky as if there was something to be seen up there. Bigman looked up. He saw nothing unusual, no clouds, not even a hawk circling. The young man took a deep breath.

Look, Auntie, I know you think that by living up here you can keep them out. But you can't. No one is coming to help you with this. You're alone. That's just the way it is these days. All that other stuff of yours, little people, giants, spirits that will protect the land . . . Auntie, it is all in the past. You're just one old woman they can push aside. No one is here to help you.

The smile was gone from the old woman's face.

Oh. Really.

The old woman stood up. Bigman knew what she was going to do. He knew that he should slip away. But then he looked down at his feet. He sighed.

Where you going, Auntie?

The old woman walked straight to the bushes where Bigman was concealed. She held out her hand. Bigman sighed again, then held out his finger. The old woman took hold and, as Bigman rose to his feet, started down the slope again, towing him behind her the way a small child pulls along a grown-up who has agreed to play.

The young man stood there, staring up.

Sacre bleu. Mother of God. Jesus Christ.

Mind your manners.

The young man's mouth was wide open, but Bigman decided it was not a threat since he was not showing his teeth. Just to be certain, though, Bigman showed his teeth a little when he smiled.

Still think I'm alone?

The young man stared at Bigman. Then his eyes drifted down to Bigman's feet.

You made those, didn't you? You made moccasins for a . . .

Friend.

Auntie, are you crazy? No, maybe I'm crazy. I'm imagining this. This isn't real.

The young man held up a hand toward Bigman. Taking it as a friendly gesture, Bigman reached out a finger and prodded the young man in the chest with it. The young man staggered back.

Real enough for you, nephew?

The young man took a deep breath, opened his mouth, and then closed it. He did it again. It was a behavior Bigman had not seen before. He did the same, opening his mouth wide and then closing it again.

Auntie, this isn't funny. He is eight goddam feet tall, covered with hair and naked except for those moccasins. Look at his teeth. Do you think he just eats roots with teeth like that? Auntie, those are for eating meat. You know what they say that . . .

People.

That . . . people like him eat.

Those are just old stories.

Auntie, you are the one who told me those stories.

The old woman let go of Bigman's finger. She turned, stepped back and looked up at Bigman.

You hear what he said.

Bigman looked down at her.

Well, you ever eat anyone?

She held up her hand and made biting motions along it, ending at her wrist and then swallowing. She looked at him.

Bigman put his head down like a little child caught taking food from the kill before the older ones had motioned him in. He looked up at her with his eyes, keeping his head down. Then he spread his arms out and shrugged. It had only been once . . . or twice.

Well, the old woman said. Well.

She wiped her hands on her sides as if to dry them, even though they were not wet.

Oh Jesus, Auntie.

Cigabi. Hush now. Let me tell you a story I never told you before. When I was a little girl I came up in this valley with my parents for the first time. I wandered away from them and I got lost. They couldn't find me. They thought I'd fallen off a cliff or drowned in the river. But that night, I came walking into camp. I told them that a big man had found me crying in the forest. That big man was all dressed in a hairy coat.

The old woman placed her hand on Bigman's side and stroked it. Bigman reached down and gently petted her head with his finger.

That big hairy man carried me back to the place where my parents were camped and then put me down. When I turned around, he was gone.

The old woman clapped her hands and rubbed them together.

So, you going to help me carry my things, nephew?

You're going to come out with me?

No need for me to be here anymore.

The old woman turned and grasped one of Bigman's hands in both of hers. She looked up at him and began to sing. Bigman hummed along with her. He felt sad, but he still hummed along. When the song was finished she began to speak to him.

I'll try to come back. But I have to go now. You take care of our valley.

Bigman slipped back into the forest while they were putting the old woman's things into packs. He followed through the forest, watching as they walked down the valley and took the rocky trail that led out of its mouth. He watched until they were gone. Then he kept watching.

The sun rose and set, rose and set again. The first road crew started work at the bottom of the rocky trail. That night a slide of rocks came down, burying their machinery and obliterating the work they had done. A second rock slide stopped their work halfway through the next day. A team of surveyors hiked up the trail, picking their way through the stones. When they entered the valley, a feeling of disquiet spread through the small party of men. A sound like an eagle's high whistle came from the slopes above them. The disquiet turned to alarm when the whistle became a deep-throated roar. Then the trunk of a huge dead tree came flying through the air and landed in front of them. Alarm turned to panic as they fled the valley.

Another sunrise came. The helicopter circled the valley. No spot was open enough for them to come down. A place would have to be cleared before they could land. From the air they saw no sign of whatever it was that had spooked the surveyors. They'd been listening to too many stories about this valley. Dead Man's Valley was what some of the locals called it, saying it had something to do with the old Indian stories about the place having some sort of spirit guardian. The local Indians weren't saying anything. When a news crew tried to do an interview with an old woman reputed to be a tradition bearer, her only response was one they couldn't use on the air.

It was decided by those running the survey that the animal in the valley was some sort of big bear. The sun rose and set. Four men with high-powered scoped rifles and night vision goggles went into the valley. They'd hunted most everything, these hunters. Including other men. They set up camp near a deserted shack and looked for animal tracks. Coyote, fox, wild turkey, fisher, and deer. Nothing unusual aside from what seemed to be moccasin tracks, really big ones, in the soft earth where a stream came down the hill. The lead hunter, a white South African who had spent time in Guatemala, smiled. If it was a big Indian, it would kill just as easy as a bear. He knew this from experience.

The sun rose and set, rose and set. Two men came stumbling down the trail without their rifles. Their story was too strange for anyone to believe. The other two men were never seen again. When the news crew tried again to get an interview with the old Indian woman all that she did was laugh and laugh and laugh.

The survey was abandoned. The legislature met and the lines were redrawn.

Bigman looked down into the valley. It was quiet, aside from the small curl of smoke that rose, almost like the feather of a grey goose, lifting again from the small shelter made of wood at the valley's far end. He smiled as he reached one hand down to caress the moccasins on his feet. Then he went down to see his friend.

A PANTHER IN THE ATTIC

Russell opened the door to the attic stairs. He wondered for a moment who had pulled out the nails that held it shut. Then the jerking of the leash in his right hand took all of his attention. The rawhide cord was as taut as a bowstring as the panther strained on its leash. He took a quick step forward, wrapping the leash around his hand as he did so. Now he was straddling the huge animal.

Grama Big Eel told him that was how her daddy did it when he worked with big cats in the carnival. *Straddle 'em when they walk. How the mama lion does it with her kittens. Then you are the mama. They start to get out of line you just pat 'em up the side of the head with the heel of your hand, just like a mama cat does.*

He guided the panther into the stair well. They began to climb. It wasn't easy going. The stairs were piled with dusty wooden boxes and green glass bottles. Bundles of plants hung from nails driven into the walls on both sides. Dry leaves and stalks of corn and comfrey, sage and goldenrod, jewelweed and mullein, rustled against his bare arms as they worked their way up.

Getting a panther into an attic is no easy thing, he thought. *Especially seeing as how there is no attic in this house any more. Not since the fire eight years ago.* They were almost at the top when he stumbled over an empty beer bottle. His grip on the rawhide leash loosened. It slipped through his fingers as the great cat pulled free. It made one leap and then another up the stairs before turning to look back down at him from the darkness. It shook its head and then closed one eye. That one gold eye staring down at him began growing larger and larger, brighter and brighter, so bright that Russell had to close his own eyes.

When he opened his eyes again, that yellow eye was still staring down at him. It was so bright it made him blink. There was morning sun coming down hard out of the open sky over the old recliner chair. He coughed. A white cloud of his breath wreathed his face. He fumbled the blanket down off his chest, trying to find the Aviator sunglasses he'd been wearing when he collapsed out here the night before. Put them on, he thought, to block out the late October sunlight piercing his skull like an icepick. His groping hand found something hard and smooth. Wrong shape. A crushed Coors can. The rest of the six pack, all dead soldiers, were scattered on the blanket. Those kids from the college who were half his age had come to sit with him on his favorite bench on Saleen Street. Bring him a couple six packs. Hear his real Indian stories. War stories.

He vaguely remembered trying to start a fire inside the woodstove in the house. Real Indian can always start a fire. Especially one with Ranger training. Even in the rain with wet wood. Unh-hunh. He had tried using the cardboard of the six pack carton in the wood stove, but it hadn't worked. The door of the stove open, the unburned carton sitting on the dead grey ashes. Just as well. He'd gotten a fire going he probably would have burned the rest of the house down. Seeing as how he wasn't going to get it any warmer in the house, he had wrapped the remaining cans in the blanket and come out here.

Now it was time to get up. But not that easy. The recliner was permanently stuck. That was why it was out here in the cornfield, in back of the house. It'd still be here when the snow fell. Maybe he'd put a piece of black plastic over it. Make it last another year. Maybe not. He kicked the blanket free of his boots. He hadn't even taken them off last night. Then he swung his feet around and levered himself up out of the chair. First thing he did was find the sunglasses, with his right foot. He shook his head and then reached down to pick up the bent frames, and watched as the pieces of dark glass fell to the earth. Broken glass doesn't belong in a cornfield. He lowered himself to his knees and picked up each of the glittering black shards and piled them in the plam of his right hand. One lance-shaped piece of lens was streaked with bright red. He looked at his left thumb. Blood was oozing out of the cut, made as clean as a razor. He dropped the pieces of glass into the coffee can he kept by the recliner for his cigarette butts. Then he squeezed his thumb hard so that more blood flowed, holding his hand out as he did so. The blood fell onto the fingery roots of a tall yellowing corn plant.

As he walked toward the house, the throbbing in his head got worse. His stomach felt as if it had been pulled out and put back in upside down. The old need-another-brew feeling. But not this morning. Not after that dream.

He stopped fifty yards from the house and cocked his head as he looked at it, trying to see the way it was. His brother Forrest and he had done a decent job, sawing, sanding, patching and re-roofing. Taking away the charred beams and the scorched shingles. Fire department never comes here. The whole place would have gone if it hadn't been for that thunderstorm, that rain that had come down so hard it just snuffed out the flames. Didn't surprise Grama Big Eel at all. Seeing as how she had asked for that rain.

He continued on, dropping the blanket with the beer cans in it into the corner as he entered the open back door. And there was the door. Still nailed shut. A door that you can't open. And even if you could get through, it led you nowhere. Just like most of the doors around the rez.

Russell shook his head as he looked at the door. *How the hell,* he thought, *am I going to get that damn panther out of my attic?*

The earth shook under his feet. One. . . two . . . three. And then the thunder of the blast came rolling down the valley.

"Deer Haven," Russell said. He had to use the outhouse.

At the Real Trading Post, Grama Big Eel was behind her counter. For half a century now she had been selling groceries and souvenirs from her log cabin store. With those groceries you had to be careful what you bought. Some of the things on her shelves, especially on the north wall, were more for decoration than for eating. Deliveries to her place weren't all that regular. The shops just on the boundary line of the reservation, the ones that sold tax-free cigarettes, they had delivery trucks pulling up to them every day. They also had pumps doing regular business with people willing to come a few miles off the interstate to get gas cheap. But those shops didn't sell booze. No one could sell alcohol legally on the reservation and this year even the bootlegger by Toad Swamp wasn't selling that much. The Tribal Council had been cracking down on selling booze this year. Making up for what they weren't doing or about to do.

Grama Big Eel didn't sell cigarettes anymore. It wasn't just that she didn't want to deal with the Tobacco Warriors, smugglers and unhappy federales. She read a lot. Anyone who visited her knew that. Two days ago she'd made Russell sit down at her kitchen table while she shared some of the statistics with him. "50,000 people every year killed by that second-hand smoke. You hear that, Russell Painter?" She looked at him over the top of her bifocals as he shifted his Camels to the backpocket of his jeans.

Only souvenirs Grama Big Eel sold were real. So real that they almost made your heart ache. No Japanese stuff. Real stuff like Gary Planter's small water drums, John Tree's wood carvings, and sometimes even a flute, Lillian Mink's porcupine quill earrings, and so on. The other real stuff in her store was local, too. All on the shelves on that same west wall of her store where you found the souvenirs. Or maybe in baskets on the floor. Fresh vegetables and fruits. Home-canned goods that vanished anytime someone white with a suit on walked in. Sometimes the Board of Health got bored enough to actually send someone out to the rez. Or maybe someone from Fish and Game, who'd heard that the freezer in the back of the store was stocked with illegal deer meat and other wild game but never found anything but that one very old, very freezer-burned turkey when they looked.

Grama Eel's real things sold. So much so that sometimes there would be nothing at all on those shelves on the west wall except those postcards showing Grama as a young woman. Standing with her mother and grandmother in front of the cabin, all three proudly holding up bolts of calico trading cloth given them by the state. It was in the old treaty that every family would get a bolt of calico cloth every year. For more than sixty years the state had been trying to convince the people to take money instead. People like Grama Big Eel who would listen patiently to all their logical arguments about doing it differently, and then say, "So, next year maybe you will bring a different color cloth, eh?"

Whether her shelves were empty or full, it didn't matter to Grama Big Eel. "I don't run this place for my health," she said. That was true. Not for her health.

She held up a small brown bottle as Russell came through the door. "These will help," she said. "Organic, multiples, lots of Vitamin C."

Russell dropped a dollar onto the counter and held out his palm. Grama Big Eel made the dollar vanish and dropped fifty cents in change and six gel-caplets into his hand all in one easy motion. The two quarters were placed eagle-side up. It was the same way she always handed bills to people, eagle-side up. The other side shows the face of a white man. You can't always trust a white man. You can always trust an eagle.

Grama Big Eel thumped the glass bottle that she kept on the floor up onto the counter top and pulled out the cork. She poured the water into a glass that had a blue jumping buffalo and the words BILLS FAN stencilled on the side. Bubbles rose from the bottom and clung to the sides of the glass. Water from the mineral spring at the base of Turkey Hill on the eastern edge of the rez, where Deer Haven was.

Russell looked hard at the old woman. She was leaning on the counter, her gaze away from him, out the window. Innocent as a baby. He tossed the pills into his mouth. The water was surprisingly cold, but it went down as if melting something out of his throat, out of his chest. His head began to feel clear and the greyness went from his vision. In spite of himself, he smiled.

"Damn."

"No way they can bottle that water," Grama Big Eel said. "No way they can take it off our land. Have to drink it the same day you get it. Got to leave something in exchange."

"Like dynamite?" Russell growled. "What do we give them back in exchange for that?" He didn't know why he said it. He didn't even know he'd been feeling angry.

Grama Big Eel caught him with her eyes. It was like having a big man grab you by the collar with both hands and then lift you off your feet.

"No," she said. "That is not the way. You don't stop anything by hurting people."

Russell tried to ask her what she meant. But her eyes dropped him. Grama Big Eel shifted her weight on the stool. The stool creaked in protest. "My legs," she said, "they are not so good as they used to be. Just look at them."

It was a flirting sort of thing to say. Russell tried not to smile at the way she was changing the subject and teasing him and boasting all at the same time. Grama Big Eel's legs were just fine. You saw that when she danced. Her legs were as good as those of her granddaughters. As good-looking, too. Well, as good-looking as most of them.

"Millie been asking about you," Grama Big Eel said. "She wonders when you going to write her there at that school."

Damn! How did she always know what he was thinking? Russell didn't answer her. There was no way to answer. He walked over to her wood stove, opened it up, stirred the coals with the poker, and then put a log in. Someone tapped on the wall of the cabin. Grama Big Eel called out the old Indian word that held both blessing and greeting in its two syllables.

Marion Smoke came in. She nodded to Russell. Nodding was a big improvement. He nodded back. Marion hadn't even looked at him for the last two weeks. Her husband Joe and he had both served together in the Gulf. It had been the anniversary of Desert Storm. He'd kept Joe out too late that Friday night. When they came back, it was so late that Joe decided not to go in the house and maybe wake her up. So Russell had helped him bunk down in his cousin's boat parked out front on the trailer fastened to the back of Bill's pick-up. It wasn't fair that Marion blamed him for that. It was Joe's idea to sleep it off in that damn boat. Joe always was a sound sleeper, even when the Scuds were coming in. Wasn't his fault that Joe Smoke slept so sound. And it sure as hell wasn't his fault that Bill Smoke decided to leave before dawn to go for the salmon run on the lake.When Joe woke up a hundred miles away there was no way he could take Marion shopping at the new mall like he had promised.

"Nice morning for blasting," Marion said.

Grama Big Eel shook her head and poured a glass of spring water for Marion.

As she drank the water Marion looked over at Russell, who was crouched down by the fire. "Your brother still down there in DC?"

Russell nodded.

"Think he'll get them to decide anything before Hell freezes over?"

"I don't talk to him that much."

Marion turned back to Grama Big Eel. "Quart of milk, dozen of those fresh eggs. Otherwise no breakfast for Joe and the boys." She thumbed open her purse. "You think we are ever going to get it together like those Onondagas. Someone was trying to pull something like that on them, there'd be two roadblocks up by now."

"We just need someone to get it started here," Grama Big Eel said. "Anyhow, we got Forrest in Washington."

"Hunh," Marion said. "He's the only one."

Russell put another log into the fire.

Russell sat by the fire as people came and went. It was a typical Sunday morning. People picking up a few things or just exchanging a little gossip. Grama's Real Trading Post was like the heart of the community. Everything flowed through it, like the soft, steady drum pulse that kept the mind and body alive. The only people who didn't knock first and hear that greeting in Indian were outsiders: a white couple looking for a Sioux headdress (they didn't find one) and an immaculately dressed African-American man with graying hair (turned out to be a Jehovah's Witness). The white couple were the only ones who didn't accept a glass of spring water. Around eleven, things got quiet. The church-goers were at church. The malls ten miles away were also open for worship now. It'd be another two hours before those who slept late on Sunday morning were up and about.

Russell pushed another log into the stove. He felt a prickling at the base of his neck. He turned around and looked. Grama Big Eel was standing there, straight up to her full height of close to six feet. Her hands were raised high over her head. She slowly lowered both hands toward Russell.

"Just stretching," she said.

"That is an eagle feather in your hand."

"This old thing here?" She looked at the feather in her hand, turning it as if she hadn't noticed it before, as if it had just flown down and landed on her like a fly. "This is just a goose feather with the tip painted black. Tommy Buffalo makes these. You seen me sell a hundred of these. Four dollars, no tax."

"That is no goose feather," Russell said. "Why is it all beaded if it is some goose feather? What are you doing to me?"

Grama Big Eel walked behind her counter and opened something out of Russell's sight. She whispered a few words he couldn't hear and then put the feather away.

"You sent me that dream."

Grama Big Eel looked down at him. She raised one eyebrow. "What dream? How would I know you been dreaming about some panther?"

Russell felt as if a handful of snow had been dropped down the back of his neck. He stood up and walked to the counter and looked up at the tall old woman. He was about 5'9", but she still towered over him. When he was just a kid, he always thought of her and Turkey Hill at the same time. As if she and that hill and that old sacred spring were one being. She was always giving people water from that spring. The bottle under her counter was always full. Had he ever seen her getting water from the spring?

She filled the glass with spring water and handed it to him. His hand trembled as he drank it.

"You and Forrest," she said. "You are the last two of your family. Brothers like Day and Night are brothers. Other families here are big, but the Painters have always been few. And they have always fought for our people. That is why you came back here, even though you are too stubborn to admit it. Maybe it scares you, too. So you didn't want to admit you amount to something. You with your drinking. Fooling yourself. Grandson, you know what your name means."

Russell put his hands down on the counter and looked at them. Broad hands, just like Forrest's. Short strong fingers, almost like paws. *Painter means panther. Pulling myself up into the attic, back into the past.*

"There's no use," he said. "Forrest isn't going to make it in time. They won't have a decision for weeks. By then they'll have the roads and the foundations in. They'll have drilled the wells and filled in the spring. They won't stop a big development like Deer Haven then, even if we do prove it is really on our land and not off the reservation like their crooked surveyors and their bribed politicians say. We might get some money out of them, but we'll never get that land back."

Grama Big Eel laughed. "You and Forrest are day and night. I know what you have been dreaming." She reached under the counter and lifted up a small, heavy bag. "I got a deal on this," she said. "This aquarium sand. Too bad I don't have no aquariums. Maybe I will sell it to you."

Russell put the two quarters she'd handed him back onto the counter. Eagle side up. "That enough?" he said.

Grama Big Eel made the two quarters disappear. "How many trucks and bulldozers they park up there at night?" She pulled a camouflage backpack out from under her counter.

"Fifty," Russell said.

"I was wondering, is it true that sand will do some big damage if it gets into a fuel tank?"

"Enough," Russell said. "You know they have fences, security guards up there at night. That is what some college kids told me, they are in this Friends of the Earth group. I was out with them last night."

Grama Big Eel stopped piling the bags of sand into the back pack. "Is there anything security guards don't see?"

"A panther," Russell said. "A dream."

GROWING SEASON

Long ago, Grandmother said, One-Who-Changes decided to make the first human beings. Back then there was stone everywhere, so that was what the first humans were made from. They were shaped just as The People are shaped. They had arms and legs, hands and feet, bodies and heads. Like us they had eyes to see the world around them. But their hearts were also made of stone. They had no love or sympathy for the other living things. So, One-Who-Changes broke those first humans up again into stone. Then the real human beings, our ancestors, were made. They were made from the ash trees so that their hearts would always be growing and green, so that their feet would always be rooted in this land.

That's the story my grandmother told me. I think of it more these days and smile—a very small and brief smile, for smiling does get noticed—at the irony. Rooted my people may have been in the land, but we've always loved to travel. That's why some of my ancestors ended up guiding the Frenchmen west (where we gave our names to rivers a thousand miles from Ndakinna) and traveling across the wide salt waters to the land of dead rivers and no trees and too many people. Even my storyteller grandmother traveled far. It was on Luna 4 Colony that I first heard our origin myth from her—where the only trees to be seen, aside from the faint glow of green when the blue earth rose in the airless sky, were in the hydroponics pods.

As far as my ancestors might have gone, even the 240,000 miles to the moon, I've flown farther than all their journeys combined. I've particled past even the most distant imagined shores, thanks mostly to the way Smith and Logah discovered a way around the old physics, the bound and rebound of accelerated sub-atomic bodies carrying immeasurable mass far past—or, more accurately, around—the speed of light. But, after twenty years, the tale of their discovery and their all too successful first experiment that left us detailed notes and absolute proof of the practicality of easy interstellar travel (and two small charred holes in the floor where the two scientists had been standing) is such an old story for everyone that I won't repeat it. Instead, there is a new story, a tale still telling itself. Although, as my left wrist throbs a warning, I realize that I will have to wait until later to continue this narrative. I tap the subdermal implant four times with a fingertip and the current hour glows from the glass-smooth rectangle of brown skin. 3200 hours. Mid-day. Time for my guard shift with the Greenies.

4000 hours. I've pulled my 8 hours and I'm back in my rack. Here on the fourth planet of K-Vega-7 days are twice as long as on Prime. All that light. Light enough to draw forests up from the soil like those no living human had ever seen. Forest like those once so thick across the belly of our old Turtle Island that awed Europeans wrote of how a squirrel (deranged, tireless, and with nothing else to do for a lifetime or two) could travel from ocean to ocean, tree to tree, and never touch the ground. A world of trees is K-Vega-7. Treeworld. Its trees are so much like our old trees, though unique species, of course, that the theory of the dominance of carbon-based lifeforms in the universe is proven once again. (Forget about the silicaceous metal-eating amoeboids of Rigel 4. After eating our space ships, they deserved to be nuked. Who wants to go there, anyway?)

And there are also the indigenous ones, the Indis, the ones we all call Greenies. Human-shaped, human-sized, bi-sexual (oh my, yes) and pleasingly proportioned with the right number of eyes, ears, noses, and so on. Expressive faces showing, at just the right moments, the equivalents for human curiosity, friendship, happiness . . . pain and sorrow. Very humanlike, indeed. Although there are a few internal anomalies still being carefully studied—and you know what it takes to carefully study any (formerly) living being—it was eventually concluded that they are people, which temporarily depressed the market shares in slave trading. I'm joking, of course, about them being made slaves. Instead, they have been taken into stewardship to be trained and guided wisely, aside from the small resistant proportion (about 48%) of the population which requires incarceration. Excuse me. Protective care.

This century, while forward looking, is a firm one. So the media informs us with absolute sincerity. Individual rights must be weighed against the good of the greater whole. Take trees, for example. And we certainly did. Cheap, easily transported wood to satisfy the nostalgic needs of the many for furniture, the warmth of wood in building materials, even wood to turn into pulp for paper. The viewscreen has yet to replace the nostalgic human love for real books produced on demand just by keying in the right code for the title you wish to be printed and bound on your home Bookmat—like those in our barracks, the ink of our stories spidering out into dark shapes on good local paper. And when the Greenies tried to stop us from cutting down their forests, however inefficient they may have been at effective violence, I do not have to tell you where the weight came down. For the greater good. And though their skin was green from the chloroplasts which made it possible for them, like their trees, to get much of their food from K-Vega-7 light itself, the hemaglobin in their circulatory systems resulted in red blood under the bulldozer treads. Though there are no grave markers, I can see the large bare stretches of earth just beyond our barracks where those first forests were clear-cut and the bodies of the Indis were buried in the golden soil.

I wasn't here then. I arrived five years after pacification. But I still heard the stories from the old hands. Some told them without laughing. Some were still sick at heart, despite the greater good. But, though the Greenies had learned to speak our language as quickly as a child adopted by a foreign family, none of my fellow officers ever talked with our well-protected charges. I was the first.

The compounds where they were kept have trees in them. Not an act of weak-minded sympathy on our parts, I hasten to add. It was discovered rather early on that the Greenies sicken and die when separated from the sight and touch and scent of their trees. The longest observed survival time (again, after rigorous study) of an indigenous humanoid away from its glade was 96 hours. The trees, on the other hand, survived quite well without the Greenies. The quickly growing forests transported to and transplanted on Prime are evidence of that. They are now almost large enough to support a good-sized population of Greenies, who will, I am certain, be much in demand for Prime women and men.

During my shift, I am usually the one whose job it is to "walk the glade." Some get nervous walking among the Indis, even though violence doesn't seem to be a part of the Greenie agenda. Guilt, my grandmother always said, is one of the prime ingedients in any recipe for fear.

On one such walk Old Nest Woman greeted me from the place where she sat on a bench-shaped buttress root.

"Brown Woman," she said. Then she smiled and placed her palm against my cheek. They can't help it. They have to touch people. I nodded, but I didn't smile back. The brass get upset when they see you smiling back at the Greenies. They call it fraternization, which is not what they call what happens between our men and the Greenies women who are brought to the barracks every night. But the Greenie women don't complain. If anything, they encourage it. Unlike my own ancestors, the Eee'doss'ukh don't seem to be susceptible to any of the diseases humans carry. Aside from brute force, the only thing that seems to hurt the Eee-doss'ukh is to take them away from their forests. When they have their forests, all they need to live is a little water and now and then some of the local fruits which contain complex carbohydrates and a high complement of vitamins. Such fruits have been part of human diets here and on Prime for a decade.

"Green Woman," I whispered back. I did it in their language, which no one else has seemed interested in learning since the impeccably qualified team of PASA linguists declared it to have been fully recorded and studied seven years ago.

Old Nest Woman touched my wrist. "What do your numbers say about our day?" she asked. Her voice held an undertone of laughter. The Eee-doss'ukh have grasped more about us than most of us realize. Our strange, prime-based ways of measuring time, our religion of science, our well-hidden insecurities.

"3400 hours," I said, answering her in English.

Her smile became broader. She began a motion with her left hand but stopped just before completing a circle. "We say that now it is this close to the growing season."

"It is well?" I said in Eee-doss'ukh. That is a greeting, a way of saying thanks, even a response when someone says something you don't fully understand—as was the case right now.

"Very well, little sister," Old Nest Woman answered. "Very well."

1200 hours. Four earth days later. Too busy to keep my journal until now, and after this there will be no need for it. Yesterday Old Nest

Woman made the circling gesture again, but this time she completed it. "Dawn," she said. "At dawn all will be very well."

I looked, as I look each morning, toward the rising ball of light. I sang an old prayer that our Lenape people were given even before we had language, a thanks for all life that needed no words. Then I saw something. There, rising from the bare earth, rising from the graves of those who were planted there, were trees. No one else was up yet as I went out barefooted to walk in that new forest. The trees were as tall as I was, and had grown that swiftly overnight. In fact, they were still growing, moving and dancing as they did, even though I felt no wind. I held my hands up toward the rising sun and saw clearly what I thought I had only imagined before. The brown of my skin was now tinted with green.

Was it the touch of the Eee-doss-ukh, the fruit that we—and all of the earthpeople here and on Prime—have been eating, or something else that entered us, began to change us, will continue the change in this growing season? I think my grandmother would have had something to say about all this, and I feel her spirit with me this morning. When I open the gates of the compound and release the Eee-doss'ukh, I may ask Old Nest Woman to explain it to me. Or perhaps I will not. But before I do so, I will bury all of the books from our barracks library in the golden soil of K-Vega-7. It is the growing season. The old strong stories of trees are ready to sprout above human words.

BONE GIRL

Old Man Thomson was well known throughout the reservation. His drinking and his flirting with the younger women—who were embarassed by this old man who refused to act as an elder should act—were legendary. Many a night, his people warned him about his ways.

"Why don't you all just mind your own business? I'm not bothering anybody!" he would say when confronted.

But, as the people on his reservation knew, Old Man Thomson was most definitely bothering people. His actions bothered the young women he harassed and those who had to carry him home in a drunken stupor. Most of all, the way he behaved bothered his wife. She was filled with shame and grief from his actions and the many sleepless nights she spent wondering if he was even still alive.

"He wasn't always this way," she said. "He never used to to drink before he lost his job when they had those layoffs. And when our son was killed in that war, he just seemed to lose faith in things. That's when he started to drink. He stopped going to the longhouse and taking part in the ceremonies. And now he's just forgotten the way we are supposed to live. He's forgotten our old ways."

Perhaps she was right. But whatever his reasons for his drinking, Old Man Thomson never talked about them. And the way he acted just kept getting worse.

"It just isn't right for him to be that way," people said. "Sooner or later, something is going to happen."

One cold October night, something finally did happen. As he stumbled down a deserted road a little past midnight, Old Man Thomson was in his usual state. A half—empty bottle of whiskey was in his hand as the full moon illuminated his path. His feet shuffled through the freshly fallen leaves as a light breeze gently swayed the bare tree limbs above him.

"Can't an old man ever have any fun?! Everybody is always buttin' into my business!!" he yelled up at the moon. Then he took another swig from his whiskey bottle.

Slowly, the clouds above began to block the moon's light. With every step Old Man Thomson felt the darkness closing in around him. Soon, he could hardly see the road now. As he stopped to let his eyes adjust, he noticed something moving along the road ahead of him. Although it was very dark, when he squinted his eyes he could just make out the shape. It looked to be human.

"Who's there?" he said in a loud voice. There was no response.

"Trying to scare an old man, are ya? Leave me alone. I ain't bothering anybody." Again, there was no answer, but he could see the shape a little more clearly now. It seemed to be a woman.

Old Man Thomson started forward. He was eager now to see who it was. As he got closer, he saw that it was indeed a female. She appeared to be a young girl, though her face was turned away from him. She was wearing a long dress.

"Excuse me," Old Man Thomson said. "Would you like some company on this dark night?"

The woman didn't respond. Instead, she kept walking several yards ahead of him. What little light showed through the clouds allowed Old Man Thomson to see how the slender young woman was dressed. Almost no one dressed that way any more. She had on an old style leather dress with high laced-up moccasins. Her long black hair swayed around her shoulders in the cold wind. She didn't look like anyone he knew.

"One of those hippie girls, aren't ya?" Old Man Thomson said with a smile. There was still no answer.

"Wait up a minute. I just want to talk with you," he said.

But the girl continued her pace, more than an arm's distance ahead. On she went, Old Man Thomson close behind, further and further down the dark road until she came to the entrance to the old quarry. Without pausing or looking back, she turned into the quarry. There was a place where the rock had been carved out of the hill in such a way as to make a sort of stone bench. She sat down there, her face still turned away. Then she motioned for Old Man Thomson to come and sit beside her.

"Ahh, I knew you'd come around," Old Man Thomson said while walking toward the stone bench. Meanwhile, a sliver of moonlight began to make its way through the clouds.

"Let me get a look at your pretty face," he said, sitting down beside her. But, before he could get a look, she turned further away. Her long hair gently swished across Old Man Thomson's face.

"Playing hard to get now, are ya? It's not nice to tease an old man you know," he said, inching closer.

"How can I give you a kiss if I can't see your face?" he said, putting his hand on her shoulder. The girl did not respond.

"Come on, all's I want is a little kiss!" he persisted. More and more moonlight was shining down. Slowly, the girl began to turn her head toward Old Man Thomson. But her long glistening hair still hid her face.

"Now I'll see your pretty face," he said, putting his whiskey bottle in his pocket. Old Man Thomson brushed the hair from the girl's face just as the moon came out fully from behind the clouds.

"AAAHHHHHHHHHHHHH!!!!!!!!" Old Man Thomson screamed in horror. The moonlight showed no face at all, only a gleaming naked skull.

"Get away from me!" he screamed while scrambling backwards off the stone slab as the bone-faced girl moved closer and closer. Then there was only darkness.

The next morning, Old Man Thomson woke up in the ditch in front of his house. Slowly, he stood up. Reaching into his pocket he took out the whiskey bottle and poured its contents onto the ground. Then he walked toward his front door. For the rest of his life, Old Man Thomson never had another drink or treated any woman disrespectfully. From then on, he worked only to be a good neighbor and an even better husband. He began to attend the ceremionies and help out at the longhouse. And the people of the reservation grew to respect and honor him as an elder who understood the right way to live. The old ways had found him again.

THE HUNGRY ONE

Long ago, five people lived together in a wigwam near the River of Many Rapids. There were two small children. The boy's name was Kinosis and his sister was called Azonis. They were cared for by their loving parents, Mitongwis, the father, and Nigawes, the mother. These parents worked hard to care for their family. The fifth person who lived with them was their father's brother. All that he ever wanted to do was sleep and eat. So they called him Lazy Uncle.

Each morning, their father would go hunting. Soon after that, their mother would go to look for food plants in the forest. Then the two children would gather firewood and play while their parents were gone. And what would Lazy Uncle do? He would sit in the wigwam, close to the fire where there was food in the cooking pot. His job was to look after the children, but in truth all he ever did during the day was sleep and eat. Every afternoon, their mother would return and start to cook; and every evening their father would return with the game he caught.

After they had all eaten, they would sit around the fire while Mitongwis and Nigawes told the old stories. The two children listened closely, for they knew there was much to be learned from the old stories. But Lazy Uncle always went to sleep before the stories were over.

One day, as Kinosis and Azonis gathered firewood near the river, they heard a little cry for help. They looked out onto the river. There, caught in a tangle of floating branches, was a little bat. It was about to drown.

"We must help that little one," said Azonis.

"I will pull that little one into shore," said Kinosis. He took a long stick, hooked the floating branches with it and did just that.

The two children freed the little bat from the tangle of branches. They placed it in the sun. Soon it was warm and dry again. It looked at them and chirped in happiness. Then it jumped up into the air, circled them four times and flew away.

One morning, as always, Mitongwis, their father, left to go hunting.

"Watch over the children," he said to Lazy Uncle, who was still laying on his bed with his deerskin blanket over his head.

"I will do so," said Lazy Uncle, without moving.

Before long, Nigawes, their mother, went out to gather food plants.

"Watch over the children," she said to Lazy Uncle, who was bent over the cooking pot, scooping food out with his hand.

"I will do so," said Lazy Uncle, as he kept eating. He did not even look up when the two children, as they always did, went out to gather firewood and play.

That day, there was not as much food left in the cooking pot as usual. Before the sun was in the middle of the sky, all of the food inside the wigwam was gone. Lazy Uncle had eaten it all.

"I am hungry," Lazy Uncle said. He looked around in the wigwam, but saw nothing good to eat. He was too lazy to go outside and seek food there. Then he noticed what looked like a bone with a little meat on it. It had fallen into the glowing coals of the fire.

"That looks good to eat," Lazy Uncle said. He reached for that bone, but as he did so he burned his finger very badly.

"Ahh-heee," he said as he stuck his burned finger into his mouth to suck it. Then a smile came over his face. "This tastes gooood," he said. "I have found something gooood to eat."

Then he ate all the flesh off his finger.

"That was gooood," he said, "but I am still hungry."

Then he stuck another finger into the fire, cooked it, and ate the flesh from it.

"Yes," he said, "I have found something gooood to eat."

One by one, he cooked and ate all of his fingers. Then he cooked his toes and ate them. He cooked his arms and ate them. He cooked his legs and ate them. He cooked all the flesh on his body and ate it all until all that was left of Lazy Uncle was a skeleton.

But he was still hungry. As he looked out of the door of the lodge he saw his niece and nephew playing at the edge of the clearing. After covering himself with his deerskin blanket he called to them.

"Children," he called, in a voice that was as hard and dry as bare bones, "Come heeeere. I found something good to eeeat. Come heeere, I neeeed yooooou!"

Kinosis and Azonis looked at each other.

"Our uncle's voice frightens me," said Azonis.

"His voice sounds hard and dry as bone," said Kinosis. "We must not go into the wigwam."

So they did not do as their uncle said.

"Children," he called, again and again, "Come heeere. I neeeed yoooou." But they did not come to him. And even though he was now a hungry skeleton, Lazy Uncle was still too lazy to come out and get them.

Finally, when the sun was only the width of one hand away from sunset, Nigawes came home.

"My children," she said, "why are you not in the wigwam? It will soon be dark."

"Mother," said Azonis, "something is wrong with Lazy Uncle. He has frightened us."

Just then, Lazy Uncle's voice came from the wigwam

"Come heeeere," he called to Nigawes, "I found something good to eeeat. Now I neeed yoooou."

"Do you hear, Mother? His voice sounds very strange," said Kinosis.

"Do not be foolish," said Nigawes. "He is your father's brother. He sounds as if he is not well. I will go see what is wrong."

The children tried to stop her, but their mother did not listen. They watched as she went to the door of the wigwam and looked inside. She could see a shape wrapped up in a deerskin blanket.

"Are you ill?" she said, and disappeared into the wigwam.

The only response was a loud thud and a body falling to the ground. The fire inside the wigwam grew brighter, then all was quiet for a long while. Kinosis and Azonis held their breath. Then they heard the voice of Lazy Uncle once again.

"Children," Lazy Uncle said, "I found something good to eeeat again. But now I neeed yoooou. Come heeere."

But Kinosis and Azonis stayed where they were. They sat with their arms around each other at the edge of the clearing as night began to fall.

Just before it was completely dark, their father came home.

"My children," Mitongwis said, "Why are you out here? It is growing cold. Let us go into our wigwam by the warm fire."

"Father," said Azonis, "we are afraid of our uncle."

"His voice is hard and cold," said Kinosis. "He told us to come inside, but we would not do so. Then our mother went into our wigwam and she has not yet come out."

"Children," said Mitongwis, "do not be foolish. Lazy Uncle is my brother. Why would he want to harm us? Wait here. I will see what is wrong and then you can come inside."

The children begged their father not to go into the wigwam, but he did not listen. He walked to the door of the wigwam and looked in. The fire had burned down very low and it was hard to see.

"My brother," Mitongwis called, "where are you?"

"I am heeere," said the cold voice of Lazy Uncle. "Come inside. I neeeed yooou."

Then Mitongwis bent his head and disappeared into the wigwam. Once more, as the children held each other tight, they heard a loud thud and the sound of a body falling. Then, as the fire burned brighter, all was quiet for a long time. Finally, they heard the hard dry voice of Lazy Uncle.

"Children," Lazy Uncle called, "I found something good to eeeat. But I am hungry again and I neeeed you. Do not come heeeere. I am coming out to get yoooou."

Frozen with terror, the children watched the door of the wigwam. They heard a sound like the sound of dry bones scraping together.

Tsschick-a-tsschick
Tsschick-a-tsschick
Tsschick-a-tsschick
Tsschick-a-tsschick

Then a tall pale shape came slowly out of the door. The moonlight glistened off its skull and its bare bones. As the hungry skeleton that had been their uncle straightened up, the two children could see its eyes gleaming like green flames. Its teeth were covered with blood.

"Children," the hungry skeleton said, "I am coming to get yooou."

Tsschick-a-tsschick
Tsschick-a-tsschick
Tsschick-a-tsschick
Tsschick-a-tsschick

He began to walk toward them. The two children jumped up and began to run, with the hungry skeleton right behind them.

Tsschick-a-tsschick
Tsschick-a-tsschick
Tsschick-a-tsschick
Tsschick-a-tsschick

They followed the trail that led next to the River of Many Rapids. As they ran, they heard a terrible scream from behind them.

"AHHH-YAAAGGGHHH"

It was the hunting cry of the hungry skeleton. The children ran as hard as they could, but it seemed as if it would soon catch them. Just then, a little shape came flying down to flutter in front of them. It was the little bat they had rescued from the river.

"Children," squeaked the little bat, "you saved me and now I must save you. Follow me."

Then the little bat led them to the place where a huge tree had fallen across the river.

"Cross here," squeaked the little bat. "Wait on the other side."

The children ran across the log to the other side. When they turned to look back, they saw the hungry skeleton standing on the river bank.

"Children, come back to meeee," said the hungry skeleton. "I neeeed you."

"No," Azonis said. "We will not come to you."

"Come over here to us," said Kinosis.

"I will dooooo soooo," said the hungry skeleton.

Then it placed one bony foot onto the log and began to walk across.

Tsschick-a-tsschick
Tsschick-a-tsschick
Tsschick-a-tsschick
Tsschick-a-tsschick

Soon it was in the middle of the log.

"Quick! Push the log into the river," squeaked the little bat.

The two children did as the little bat said. With a terrible scream, the hungry skeleton fell into the swift water and was washed away.

"Follow me," the little bat squeaked, "It is not dead yet. It will chase you again."

The little bat flew on and the two children followed. It led them along a narrow trail that wound up to the top of the high cliffs over the river. There was a deep gorge with many sharp rocks far below. At last they came to the deepest part of the gorge. There, next to the cliff, was a small wigwam. In front of the wigwam sat a short little man smoking a pipe.

"Grandfather," the little bat squeaked, "a hungry one is chasing these children. Help them."

"Are these children good children?" said the little man.

"They saved my life," said the little bat. "I have watched them sitting by the fire and listening closely to the old stories. They are good children."

"Then I must help them," said the little man.

He put down his pipe and walked to the edge of the gorge where two trees grew close together. He wrapped one leg around one tree and one leg around the other tree. Then he leaned and leaned and leaned and leaned. Each time he leaned, his body stretched until he had reached the other side. On the other side two trees grew close together. He wrapped one arm around one tree and the other arm around the other.

"Use my back as a bridge," the little man said.

Just then, a terrible cry came from nearby.

"AHHH-YAAAGGGHH!"

"Quickly," said the little man. "The hungry one is coming up the trail. He is very close."

Kinosis and Azonis did as the little man said. They stepped onto his back to cross over to the other side. They could hear the roar of the swift water far below and they could see the moonlight on the jagged rocks. But they did not hesistate. Holding each other's hand, they crossed to the other side. As soon as the two children stepped off his back, the little man let go of one tree, then let go of the other tree. Whoooooosh, he shrank back to his normal size.

The little man had just picked up his pipe again when the hungry skeleton reached the edge of the cliff.

"Little man," said the hungry skeleton. "I sssaaaw what you diiiid. Those children are miiiine. Make it sooo that I can get them."

So the little man put down his pipe. He wrapped one leg around one tree and one leg around the other tree. Then he leaned and leaned and leaned and leaned. Just as before, each time he leaned, his body stretched until he had reached the two trees on the other side. He grabbed one tree with one hand and the other tree with the other hand.

"Now try to use my back as a bridge," he said.

"Children," said the hungry skeleton, "I am coming to get yooouuu!"

Then the hungry skeleton stepped onto the little man's back and began to walk across the gorge.

Tsschick-a-tsschick
Tsschick-a-tsschick
Tsschick-a-tsschick
Tsschick-a-tsschick

But as soon as he was in the middle, the little man let go with his hands. The hungry skeleton fell into the deep gorge with a terrible scream.

"AHHHH-YAAAGGGHHH"

It struck the sharp rocks below and shattered into many pieces.

"Children, you are safe now," the little man called over to Kinosis and Azonis. "Take that path. It will lead you home."

"But we no longer have any parents," said Azonis.

"The hungry skeleton ate them," said Kinosis.

"Children," said the little man, "is there a tall tree leaning over your wigwam?"

"Yes," said Azonis.

"That is so," said Kinosis.

"Do you remember the old stories?" said the little man. "If you do, then you know what to do."

The two children ran home as fast as they could. By the time they got to their wigwam, the sun had risen. They looked inside. All that was left of their parents were bones. But they remembered the old stories. They ran to the base of the tall tree that leaned over the lodge and began to push. As they pushed, the tree began to fall. Then they shouted the words that they had heard from the old stories.

"Mother, Father, get up quickly! A tree is about to fall on your wigwam!"

Just before the tree struck the wigwam and crushed it, their mother and father jumped out of the door. The flesh was back on their bones and they were alive and well again.

Kinosis and Azonis ran to embrace them.

"You have saved us," said Mitongwis.

"You have brought us back to life," said Nigawes.

From then on, the four of them lived there near the River of Many Rapids for a long time. Their lives were very happy.

But what about Lazy Uncle, who became a hungry skeleton? That gorge where he fell onto the rocks is still there. His bones are still there among the stones. It is said that every time someone is really greedy, every time someone is really lazy, those bones come closer together.

Some nights, they say, when you walk by that gorge, you may hear a faint sound from far below. Perhaps it is the sound of Lazy Uncle, the hungry skeleton, seeking a way to get out of that gorge.

Tsschick-a-tsschick
Tsschick-a-tsschick
Tsschick-a-tsschick
Tsschick-a-tsschick

Author's Note: The story of the greedy man or woman who becomes a hungry skeleton is widely told among the Native nations of North America. So, too, is the method of bringing bones back to life by pushing over a tall tree and shouting at them to get out of the way. This particular version of the story is based on the way the tale is told among the Western Abenaki and the Kahnawake Mohawks of northern Vermont and southern Canada. The names of the characters in the story are Abenaki names.

BAD MEAT

In the old days of the beaver trade, a Penobscot man decided to go hunting and trapping far to the north. Few people dared to go there, even though there was much game. His young wife wanted to go along.

"Take me with you," she whispered to him as they lay together in bed.

"I do not think that is a good idea," the man said. "It is dangerous in the north. There are great creatures there that hunt human beings."

"You will be cold in the north," the woman said, moving closer to him. "I can keep you warm at night."

"Ah, that is very true," the man said. "I am already warmer."

"Good, then I will come with you and I will bring my mother."

"Why must you bring your mother?" the man said.

"My husband," the woman said, moving her hands, "do not talk any more."

"Ah," the man said. Then, indeed, he did stop talking.

The next day, when the man set out to the north, his wife and his mother-in-law were in the canoe with him. They traveled for many days up the rivers, carrying the canoe around waterfalls and across portages between the different streams. At last, they reached a part of the north land where none of their people had been before. There were game animals everywhere. There were many beaver lodges in the ponds. They set up their camp beside a big lake.

Before long, the man was glad that his wife's mother had come along with them. She was a good worker. She did most of the work of making a wigwam, covering it with birch bark and making a floor of woven hemlock boughs. She gathered most of the wood for the fires and did much of the cooking. The man soon realized his mother-in-law was also quick-thinking. Whenever there was a problem, she always had an idea about what to do.

Best of all, when night came, his wife's mother went to bed early. Whenever the man and his wife climbed into their own blankets on the other side of the bark lodge, the old woman would always be sound asleep with her head covered. This pleased the man. Some of his friends had told him how difficult it was for them to be with their own wives while their mother-in-laws sat on the other side of the fire watching them with unblinking and slightly amused eyes.

The hunter soon began to bring back much game after each day's hunting and trapping. The two women skinned the animals and smoked the meat. They built another canoe of birchbark and spruce so that they could bring everything back with them. Everything was going well. One day, though, while he was out hunting, the hunter heard a strange howl from far up on a nearby mountain. Then he found large tracks in the soft earth near a stream. He hurried back to their camp by the lake.

"I have heard the howl of the kiwakwe," he said. "I have found its tracks in the earth. I think it is going to come for us. We must break camp and leave here quickly."

The kiwakwe is a giant monster. It looks like a man, but it is covered with long matted hair and its teeth are like those of a wolf. Sometimes, it is said, the kiwakwe covers its body with pine pitch. When the pitch is hard, it is like an armor that spears and arrows will not pierce. Although the kiwakwe is very stupid, it is also very dangerous. It likes nothing better than to hunt human beings for food.

As the man and his wife were packing one canoe, while the wife's mother carried the last load down to the beach, an awful howl came from the forest. The kiwakwe came running out. It saw the man and woman by the canoe first and ran down the beach toward them.

"My mother," the woman cried.

But the man pushed his wife into the canoe. He shoved it into the lake, leaped in and began to paddle madly. The kiwakwe waded after them, but it could not go into the deep water.

"Come back," the kiwakwe howled. "I am hungry."

But the man just paddled harder without looking back.

Seeing that the kiwakwe was between her and the second canoe, the old woman knew that she could not escape. However, the monster had not yet noticed her. She laid down on her back, pulled her dress over her head and spread her legs.

Soon the kiwakwe came back up the beach. It saw the old woman lying on her back with her dress over her head.

"What is this one?" the kiwakwe growled. "Is this one dead?"

The kiwakwe poked the old woman with his long finger, but she did not move.

"I wonder how long this meat has been dead," the kiwakwe said. "I wonder if it is still good."

Then the kiwakwe rubbed its finger between the old woman's legs, lifted its finger and smelled.

"Ugh," the kiwakwe said. "This meat has gone bad, it is not good to eat."

Meanwhile, the hunter and his wife had brought their canoe back close to the land far downshore from the other canoe.

"Come and eat us if you are hungry," the hunter shouted. "Look, we are here where you can catch us."

"Ahhh," the kiwakwe growled. "Wait for me. I will come and get you."

Then it ran down the beach toward the canoe of the husband and his wife. They waited until it was close to them and then once again paddled out into the lake just beyond the monster's reach.

As soon as she heard the kiwakwe move away, the old woman pulled down her dress, jumped to her feet and ran down to the other canoe. She pushed it in and paddled. By the time the kiwakwe saw her, she was too far out in the lake.

The kiwakwe was very upset. It ran down to the shore and waved at the old woman.

"Bad meat," it howled, "I am sorry. Come back, bad meat."

In reply, the old woman stood up, raised her dress and showed her backside to the kiwakwe.

Then the old woman, her daughter, and the hunter paddled away, leaving the kiwakwe behind with nothing to eat at all, not even bad meat.

BEAR SKIN ROBE

There was an old Muskogee man whose eyesight was not very good. But he knew medicine and loved nothing better than to help those who were ill. One day, he heard that there were sick people in a little settlement that was way off in the piney woods. They needed his help. So he went to his nephew who had an old Model A Ford.

"Nephew," he said, "I need to go help some people in another town. I want you to drive me. There's no other way I can get there."

"Uncle," the young man said, "why do you always help people like this? You don't do it for money. No one ever pays you."

"Nephew," the old man said, "you don't understand. When you help people in this way, they will be very kind to you." Then the old man laughed. "They have other ways of paying you. Especially the women, if you know what I mean."

"Oh," said the nephew. He did know what his uncle meant.

"If you drive me there," the old man said, "they will be grateful to you, too."

"Uncle," the young man said. "I will drive you."

So they went to the town and the old man used his medicines. His medicines were strong and soon the people who had been sick were well again. Just as the old man had said, the people didn't pay him any money but they wanted to reward him in other ways. They gave the two men a big feast and presents. The people in the town were so grateful that they asked the old man and his nephew to stay with them for a while.

"Uncle," the young man whispered, "the women have not yet thanked us."

"That is true," the old man whispered back.

Then he smiled at the people who had invited them. "We will stay with you for awhile," he said.

The people who took them in had a small house with only two

rooms in it. There wasn't much furniture because those people lived pretty much the way folks did in the old days. They even used bear skin robes for their blankets when the nights got cold. One of these people in the house was a middle-aged woman whose husband had died some time ago. Even though he had bad eyesight, the old medicine man saw that the woman was good-looking.

One day, after they had been staying in the house for a while, that woman came up to the old man while no one else was looking.

"I would like to give you something to thank you for helping us," she said in a soft voice.

"Oh," said the old man, "that is kind of you, sister."

"But I am shy," the woman said. "There are always too many people in the house. Can you meet me tonight after everyone is asleep? I can give my something to you up on the hill where the raspberry bushes grow."

"I can do that," the old man said. "But my eyes aren't so good. How will I know it is you?"

"I will have my bearskin robe on," she said. Then she slipped away from him.

That evening the old man couldn't wait until it was dark. When it seemed that everyone else was asleep, he heard the good-looking woman stir from her bed in the other room and go out the door. He waited for awhile and then left the house. The moonlight was bright, and the woman had tied white strips of cloth to mark the trail. So he was able to find his way to the hilltop.

Meanwhile, the woman was waiting for him on top of the hill. She thought she heard him approaching. She saw a dark shadow moving through the berry bushes.

"Is that you?" she said.

In response to her words, a large black bear stood up and growled at her. The woman yelled and ran away down the hill in the opposite direction.

The old man heard the woman's yell. "Oh my," he said, "she cannot wait until I get there. She is calling for me to hurry up."

When he reached the hilltop, the old man looked around. With his weak eyes, he could just make out a dark shape bent over among the bushes.

"Sister," the old man whispered, "I am here to get it."

The dark shape grunted and moved away from him a few feet.

"Ah-hah," the old man said, "she is so shy."

He unbuttoned his pants and then moved forward very slowly, so that he would not frighten her. He held out his hand.

"Hunh," he said, "I feel your bear robe. Do not turn around, sister. It is all right this way."

He moved closer. Very gently, he felt around further.

"Sister," he said, "you are very hairy, indeed."

All the people in the house below woke up when they heard the sounds and shouting from the top of the hill. Before long the old man came running out of the darkness with his clothes torn and stumbled into the house.

The next day, even before dawn, the old medicine man and his nephew drove off in the Model A Ford. As they went down the narrow dirt road, the old man looked nervously out the window.

"Don't stop," he kept saying. "Can't you go any faster, nephew? I think there is a female bear following us."

SOJY VISITS HIS FRIENDS

One day, Sojy was out walking around. He was feeling bored.

"It has been too long since I've visited my friends, the longhouse people. I am sure that they have missed me. I must go and see them and make their lives more interesting."

So Sojy went walking along until he came over a hill and looked down on a village of the White Stone People. The village was surrounded by many tall elm trees. The men of that village all had long hair. He watched from the forest as the young men combed their hair with bone combs. He could see how vain these young men were about their hair, how they tried to impress the women of the village with their good looks.

"This is good," Sojy said. "I see how I can help them."

Then Sojy spat on his hands and began to comb his hair with his fingers. His hair got longer and darker as he combed it. When he walked into the village, all of the young men immediately noticed his hair. It was longer and shinier and better looking than any man's hair they had ever seen before.

"Stranger," the young men said. "*Sehkon*. You are welcome to our village."

"*Sehkon*," Sojy said. "My name is Long Hair."

"You hair is very long, indeed," one of the young men said. "What did you do to make your hair so long and beautiful?"

"My friends, since you have been so kind to me, I will tell you a secret. To make your hair look different than it does now, all you have to do is climb way up in a big elm tree. Tie your hair to one of the top branches and then jump. Do you have any big elm trees around here?"

All of the young men were pleased.

"We have many big elm trees."

"We will go and do as you say."

"We will do it right now."

"Un-hunh," Sojy said. "Your hair will soon look much different. But now I must go, for I have other people to help."

None of the young men noticed as Sojy walked out of the village. They were all climbing the elm trees. Just before Sojy reached the top of the hill, he stopped to listen. Soon he heard many loud screams.

Sojy nodded to himself. "I am sure their hair looks very different now." Then he continued on his way. He walked along until he came to a village of the Marshy Land People. He looked down on the village from a hill. He could see that there were many good-looking women in the village.

"It is clear," Sojy said to himself, "that these people need my help."

So Sojy dressed himself as an old medicine man and walked down the hill toward the village.

"People of the Marshy Lands," he cried loudly. "A great sickness is coming to your village. Unless something is done, many will grow ill and many will perish."

Hearing his words, the people became alarmed. Everyone gathered around him.

"Wise one," they asked, "what can we do to prevent this sickness?"

"There is only one thing that can be done," Sojy said. "But it is a hard thing to do and it will take much effort."

"Whatever it is," the people said, "we will do it."

"My children," Sojy said. "you are so brave that I, too, will do this hard thing with you."

"Grandfather," the people said, "we are honored. Now tell us what must be done."

"To prevent this great sickness," Sojy said, "we must make medicine in this way. All of the younger women must sleep with the older men and all of the older women must sleep with the younger men. As you can see, I am a very old man, so I will be the first to sacrifice myself in this way."

The people took Sojy to a lodge and he went inside to begin making medicine. The people could tell that it was a hard thing for him to do. His groans and shouts could be heard all over the village.

"If this wise old man can sacrifice himself in this way to help our people," the people said, "we must prove ourselves to be as brave as he is." Then they, too, began making medicine.

As Sojy had said, this medicine was hard and took much effort. It took many days. At last, Sojy crawled out of the lodge. He was weak and worn out from all the hard work he had done. But there was a big smile on his face.

"People," Sojy said, "the medicine has worked.The great sickness will not come to your village. Now I must go on my way to help others."

Everyone was happy. "You are the best medicine man we have ever met," many of them told him. They were sorry to see him go and all of the people thanked him when he left.

"Come back again if you hear of another such sickness," the older women told him.

Then Sojy traveled on. He visited more of his friends, but that is a story for another day.

PART TWO

SEEING THE CIRCLE:

THE WISDOM OF NATIVE STORIES

Chan K'in was a Lacandon Mayan elder said to be over 120 years old. His people live in the small patch of rain forest remaining in the Chiapas region of Mexico. When I visited him in 1992, he told me that the roots of all things are bound together and that when the last of the great trees fall, we humans will not be able to survive for long. In one of the stories he told me, one of the hundreds of traditional stories he has preserved, a man is angered because the animals of the forest are stealing his crops. He prays to be turned into a jaguar so that he will be able to drive the worthless animals from his fields. His wish is granted. He becomes a great jaguar, but as he patrols the edges of his field he sees many starving people in the forest.

"Come in, my relatives," he says, taking pity on them. "Eat all you want. I am just defending my field from those useless animals."

And from that point on none of the humans from that man's village are ever able to come near that field again as it is guarded by a great jaguar which drives away the humans and allows the animals to come in.

That is a story about vision. Like so many of the traditional stories which have been preserved and offered to us by Native elders all over the world, it reminds us that the way we see things can affect everything. It also reminds us that we, as human beings, often see only one small aspect of the reality and the worth of the natural world. Becoming a jaguar means that you will see as a jaguar sees—and that is not the same way a human views the world. It is necessary for all of our survival that we learn—if only through such powerful stories as that of Chan K'in—some small inkling of what it is to see as a jaguar.

Native stories remind us that all of life is a great circle. Where we are today, we will be again at some coming moment. This concept of the circle, which is so clearly revealed to people close to the earth by the ever-repeating rhythms of the seasons, remains remarkably foreign to the Western-based global political culture and economic systems which dominate the world. In the Western view, we progress in a straight line. It is, we are told, the shortest distance between two points. To "go forward" is a positive thing; to "get ahead" is our goal. But when we do this, what do we leave behind? And is it truly left behind or simply transformed from something which sustained us into something which will poison us or our children? We see the short-sightedness of the Western view becoming more visible every day. I pick up a newspaper, and find in it accounts of disastrous fires in California, the weakening of Federal air quality standards, and a scientific study of global warming which concludes that the process is accelerating. Each of these news items is an example of the short-sightedness of straightline thinking and of the perilous future such thinking shapes for us and our descendents. Each story also reminds me of a traditional Native tale.

There is, for example, a story told among the Pomo Indian people of California about the coming of fire. Fire was given to the human beings by the animal people, as a gift because the animals took pity on the humans which had no fur coats, who were freezing in the cold. But the humans were reminded of the power of fire, of the necessity to treat it with great respect and keep it in its proper place. The tragedy of the Oakland fire shows remarkable disrespect for the ecosystems of California, for the plants and animals, and for fire itself. Perhaps no place in North America has greater potential for wildfires than that long California coast where desert winds heading towards the ocean can roar down the canyons and over the hills with incredible force, turning sparks into a firestorm. Most of coastal California is naturally dry area, and the only way large human populations can be maintained is by taking water from somewhere else, great distances away, often at great cost to that other bioregion.

Native people, through their familiarity with the cycles of nature and the teachings kept in their stories, were aware of this danger and chose places to live with care. But the short-term priorities for builders and affluent home-owners on the California coasts were making money and having a good view. Thus, many homes were built on wooded slopes where fire danger remains great. Wooden shingles, which "look good" in the short term, but are like tinder in the dry climate of the coast, were widely used on houses which could have been built of more fire-resistant material. There was no respect shown for the power of fire with the result being tragedy. And sadly, it will happen again as more and more houses are built in such places, as the earth grows drier while water is wasted.

The current growing hole in the ozone layer—an observable reality and not a speculation—is attributed by innumerable scientists (who have their own understanding of the circularity of life and have in recent years given it the name "ecology") to human actions, the dispersal of chemicals into the atmosphere which destroy the protective layer that screens out harmful rays from the sun. Such rays can cause cancers in humans, destroy plants, and—eventually—perhaps destroy most life on earth. Fortunately, we have the ability to end this process. We, as humans, know what causes it—the release of flurocarbons through such things as air conditioners and propellants in spray bottles. Yet the changes in technology needed to end this destructive process are being resisted by the United States, apparently because of motives having to do entirely with "affordability," or financial profits and losses. We may ask what price human life is worth. (And we may be appalled to find that the U.S. government actually makes decisions on the basis of studies determining how many deaths per 1,000 as a result of such things as increased skin cancer or poisoning from checmicals in food and water can be accepted when profits are being made.) This language of economics and political expediency is so complicated and convoluted that a good story is needed which can cut through it all. Like the Abenaki story of Gluskabe and the Wind Eagle.

In this story, Gluskabe, a powerful being who lives with his wise grandmother, ties the wings of the eagle who makes the wind. He does this so that the wind will not push him back to shore when he hunts ducks. But after doing this, Gluskabe discovers that the air is stale and hot without the wind, and that the water is dirty without the waves caused by the wind, and that life without the wind is intolerable. He goes to his wise grandmother for advice. She asks him what he has done and points out to him that the wind is necessary. How, she asks him, will our children and our children's children survive without the wind? Gluskabe realizes his mistake and ends up untying the wings of the wind eagle, reversing the process to return things to the proper balance.

It is a very simple solution—but Gluskabe, who stands for all human beings in their short-sightedness—neither realizes the consequences of his actions or the results of an unwise tampering with the forces of the natural world. It is only by asking his grandmother, an elder wiser than he, that he is given the answer, and it is only by accepting his mistake and seeking to remedy it that things can be made right again. It is this process that the stories teach us, a process which we must follow as individuals, as leaders, and as nations. When things are wrong we must turn to the wisdom of the stories which counsel us, as do wise elders. When these stories show us our errors, we must then take the proper action. A feeling of guilt does nothing. Only action to restore the balance is the proper response.

Another of the Gluskabe stories tells how he made a net which caught all of the fish in the world. But his Grandmother Woodchuck told him this was wrong. If all the fish are caught, there will be none left for our children's children. How then can they survive? Gluskabe releases the fish and destroys his fish trap as a result of those words. Each time I think of that story today I think of the drift nets being used by the fishermen of Japan and Taiwan, that are strip-mining the ocean and catching all the fish while leaving none for their children's children. And I wish they could hear and understand that story of Gluskabe and do as he did.

A few years ago, after many years of using traditional stories to teach young people about the environment, Michael Caduto, a Vermont naturalist, and I put together a book called *Keepers of the Earth*. Combining lesson stories from a number of the original Native nations of North America with activities and scientific information, we hoped that we would reach at least a few people in the ways the old stories had reached their original audiences—by providing lessons in a form which was both memorable and enjoyable. The success of *Keepers of the Earth*, which now has more than a million copies in print, was not, I am sure, due to our brilliance but instead to the strength of the stories and the growing awareness on the part of more and more teachers and parents that something has been missing in education and in the way modern materialistic culture (which is now—with multi-national corporations and the growth of new economic powers in non-Western nations, a global culture of greed) views and misuses our environment. The title of the book comes from the "Keeper of the Game," the powerful animal spirit whose responsibility it is to care for its animal relatives and from the age-old Native concept that we do not own the Earth, but only take care of it for coming generations of life. It is an idea which has powerful reverberations for all of us. If we do not keep this earth— "for our children's children," as Grandmother Woodchuck expresses it to Gluskabe or "for seven generations to come," as my Iroquois friends express it—then we will surely lose it.

Sometimes, when I am telling traditional teaching stories, I explain to people that the stories are wiser than I am. This is not false modesty, but simple truth. The Native stories of North America, those stories which are in some cases, I believe, thousands of years old, carry the wisdom of all those years. There are innumerable instances of items of so-called "folk wisdom" which were dismissed by "scientific information" turning out to be truer than the science which at first discounted them. That folk wisdom was simply the distillation of many generations of experience. Think of it this way: if you live in a house for more than one winter, as they say in New England, you learn where the ice is going to fall off the roof. And how much will you know if you and your ancestors have lived in the same house for ten thousand years?

Long residency, though, has become the exception rather than the rule. The "pioneer spirit" of clearing the land and then moving on—leaving ecological disaster behind has long been the American way. (I find it ironic that contemporary Americans are condemning the burning and clearing of the Amazon jungles—one of the greatest ecological disasters of this century—without remembering that it is exactly what the "settlers" of America did as they moved west. Contemporary accounts in the 1700s tell of fires made from the great trees of the Ohio valley burning for months at a time and darkening the skies. It is a pattern which the United States gave to the world.) Today, most Americans live a semi-nomadic life based on their jobs. When a job is needed, they move on. As I look out of the window of the house I live in, a house I was raised in by my grandparents, I think of all the things I have yet to learn about this small piece of earth where so many generations of my family have lived. (It is the understanding of all the land holds for us and our children to come that led my mother to place the 80 acres of land across the road from us, land on which her house stands, into a conservation easement, protecting it in perpetuity from housing developments, clearcutting, or mining.) Yet many of the people I went to college with have had four addresses in as many states since graduating in 1964. And too many of them neither know nor care what has happened to the homes they left behind. Such rootlessness has made the average American less and less aware each year of where the ice—real ice or metaphoric ice—is going to fall, even if it may be on their own heads! It is hard for them to look to their elders for advice on how to live in harmony with the land. In most cases, their parents, too, have been part of this same rootlessness.

American Indian people, however, have remained much closer to their original land. They have moved less and when they have moved, they have continued to return to their original homes. As a result, they see their home not as houses or as a few acres of land, but as extended ecosystems. They see the Earth itself, an earth which is alive, as our mother. And in staying close to the original earth they also have stayed close to the stories which help them preserve the earth. How close the earth is to the Iroquois people can be seen in another commonly-used phrase—"the faces of our children are there just under the earth." Instead of seeing the earth as "dirty," ("dirt" itself has become a pejorative term in many ways in the English languages, despite the fact that the descendents of Judaeo-Christian traditions are, like Adam, originally rooted in earth) or as that dreaded last resting place where the dead are buried, (think, for example, of the Western tradition of horror stories, of the "unholy earth" of cemeteries where the Living Dead come forth at midnight, of Dracula lurking in a coffin filled with Transylvanian dirt —little wonder, then, that modern culture shows such contempt for the land) Native people see it as the source of life itself, as the source from which new generations will come.

Much has been said in some circles that we need "new stories" to help us understand this modern world, that things have changed so much that the past no longer has relevance and the old stories are stale and pointless. But those who say this clearly have no understanding of the power and the lessons which remain in the stories of the indigenous peoples—not just American Indians, but the aborginal natives of Australia, of New Guinea, of Africa—who have held onto these stories which are rooted in Native soils. Those who say that past knowledge is of no use have been too busy talking to truly listen. They do not recognize that life is a circle, and that if we travel far enough we will return to the places we thought we left behind. My own knowledge is very small compared to that of many elders, but I have learned enough to know that there is *no* contemporary problem that does not have a traditional story which can be used as a path towards understanding and healing.

In the past, many of these stories were not shared by Native elders. But attitudes have changed. The Traditional Circle of Elders, which has been hosted by the Onondaga Nation of the Iroquois and includes such important tribal leaders as Oren Lyons, brings together American Indian elders on a yearly basis to discuss the problems of contemporary survival. This Traditional Circle of Elders made a decision some years ago that for all of us to survive it was necessary to start sharing the old wisdom. The stories which are rooted in Native soil are still here and there are Native people now sharing them. But to learn, we must listen, and to listen we must close our mouths and open our ears.

THE TRUTH OF THE TELLING

My story was out walking around, an old time forest person, clothing made of moss, belt woven from treebark. Here, in the forest, is where my story camps.

We had traveled all the way across the eastern half of the country, driving from Mexico City to Veracruz and Coatzacoalas, Villahermosa and San Cristobal de las Casas. We had climbed through mountain passes, sinewed down the twisting narrow roads into deep valleys, burst onto the coastal plains to glimpse the blue waves of the Bay of Campeche. Then, turning south from the sea where the refineries of the Louisiana Coast exported, duty-free, a permanent haze above us, we had entered a clearcut, overgrazed landscape so barren that it seemed as if the life had been squeezed out of it like a lemon rind tossed aside to dry in the sun. Strange as it might have seemed to the average person from El Norte, there were plenty of familiar sights to remind us that we were still in the Age of America. Coca-Cola, Winston, Sony, Shell and Energizer were with us in every village, their names larger and brighter than the street signs that sometimes paid homage to older gods and other histories. A half-starved humpbacked cow tried to graze on a wind-deviled hillside beneath a billboard that showed a sleek woman and her smug male co-conspirator sharing an imported liquor. Only twenty years ago there had been rain forest and no road here, just a foot trail under towering mahoganies. But cattle ranches had replaced the trees, and produced export beef like that now shipped from formerly Amazonian jungles even further south to satisfy the appetites for ten billion burgers and still counting. And now this devoured land—that would have held a forest for a hundred millenia but could only support cattle for a decade—was incipient desert.

To say that it was profoundly depressing would have been as large an understatement as the observation that such so-called progress exacts a heavy price from the environment. All that was left of the great forest was a few tall dead trees, blackened by fire, scattered about on the hillsides. Straight and limbless as telephone poles, they seemed like mournful skeletons haunting the graves of their ancestors. My twenty year-old son Jesse and I looked at each other, wondering for a moment why we were here.

But then, as the land began to rise, we turned a bend in the road around a hill and something happened as magical as the fairy-tale transformation of a frog into a prince. A drop of rain hit our windshield. And then another, streaking down across the reddish dust that coated everything like a layer of powdered sugar. And through the clarity of that thin watery trail drawn across the glass, there was green.

And, as the rain cleared the dirt away and cooled the air, as we opened the windows that had been closed against the choking dust, we saw a road sign almost buried in the tangle of flowering bushes and vines. *Lacandon Reserve*, it read. For a hundred miles there had been no rain, but here it remained, the forest's moist breath. A dozen different orchids hung from the trees—ceiba, tropical cedar, guava, mahogany and many more I could not name. Flower petals turned the wet dark surface of the road into a red and gold silk tapestry.

It was that way all the way into the village of Naha. It was dark by the time we arrived and walked up the hill to the old man's thatched house. Firelight flickered from within and there was the feeling of many people inside. But only one voice could be heard, a strong voice with the cadence of music in it. It was a voice that changed as the rain forest changes, flowing first with wind and the jaguar's roar, then with the call of the howler monkey and the chatter of the parrot.

The door was open, an old sign of welcome, so we entered. There, next to the fire, Chan K'in Viejo sat, the children and the adults of the village gathered about him, all of them listening as he told a story. It was a story that held the life of the people as clearly as the rain forest kept the strength of the land. There was a battery-powered radio there, but it had been turned off. Chan K'in's story was better than that. He had heard the story first more than a hundred years ago when he was young. Now it was the time for a new generation of those who were young to hear it.

In the days to come we would sit and listen as Chan K'in told story after story in Mayan while our friend Robert Bruce whispered a translation to us. Stories of the wisdom of respecting the rain forest and its many beings. Stories of how new diseases for which there are no cures would come from the ruins of the forests if they were destroyed.

I had seen it before, the power of story to transform, to teach and to inspire. But I cannot think of another time when the contrast was as clear between the life of story, the vitality the story gives and guards, and the ultimate emptiness of the tales told by advertising, light-quick narratives holding no morality higher than corporate profit.

Of course there are many kinds of stories, as many kinds and ways of telling a tale as there are motives for telling. But when I speak of story I mean tradition. I mean the tale that has at the very least a double purpose: to entertain so that it will be heard and to instruct so that its lesson will be remembered. Stories, the stories that come from the earth and the long memories of peoples and places, know more than we storytellers do. We ignore them at our peril.

The day after our arrival in Naha, we sat across from old Chan K'in as he told his stories into my tape recorder. He began with an apology. He could not tell the stories as well as his father had, long ago. But, if we still wanted to listen to him, he would try to do his best. It was the kind of modesty that I've often encountered among Native elders, especially those who have the most to share.

"Great Lord," I said, speaking the few Mayan words I'd learned, "we are honored."

"Ah," he said. Then he nodded and smiled and spoke words that he so often repeated. *"Tsoi! Net Tsoi!"*

Good. It is good.

Then he began to speak, telling of his long life. He told how he was born before the awakening of the nearby volcano—an eruption that took place over 120 years ago. He spoke of his recent visit to the United States and the Council of Traditional Elders at Onondaga. He bemoaned the destruction of the forests around him by settlers and oil exploration. (Each time a great tree is cut, Chan K'in once said, a star falls from the sky.) And he told many stories, like this brief tale.

A small party of hunters was deep in the jungle. During the day, nothing had frightened them. They felt as if they were the masters of all that they saw. They did not know what fear was. But when night came, it was very dark and they felt the cold. Their fire was burning low. No one wanted to go out into the darkness to gather more wood. Then, so close that it seemed they could feel the hot wind of its breath, a jaguar roared. With this they knew fear. And so it will be for those who are destroying the forests and killing each other. When the great cold comes and the jaguar roars close to them in the night, then they will finally listen. Then, when the world is destroyed, they will understand.

When he finished this brief story, Chan K'in looked around at our solemn faces. Everyone was silent.

"So, the end of the world may come soon?" we finally asked.

"That is so," Chan K'in answered, nodding slowly. Then he smiled. "But if the destruction of the forests is stopped, if people stop killing each other, then the end will not come. *Net Tsoi!*"

All things, Chan K'in reminded us through his stories, are related to each other. By hearing the tales we are woven back into that ancient web of connections within our human family and between all human beings and the natural world. By remembering these stories and living them, we keep these stories alive. While loud and gaudy advertisements bombard us from every sensory direction, trying to convince us to obtain products that we probably do not need, stories whisper softly into our hearts the older, truly lasting messages, reminding us of what we need to be truly human. Reminding us what we need to survive. That is the truth of the telling. *Net Tsoi.*

AT THE END OF RIDGE ROAD:

FROM A NATURE JOURNAL

I. Two Owls

September 10, 2000

It is late on a warm September night. The small house that we now call The Camp was built forty five years ago on one of those ridges of land that swirl on relief maps like great waves of earth at the edge of the range of ancient mountains labeled on those same maps as the Adirondacks. The fifteen acres of property around this house, a few miles south of the blue line that marks the Adirondack Park, is protected by the conservation easement my wife and I donated to the Saratoga Land Conservancy. Although we purchased The Camp as a getaway from our other home, a house on a busy rural corner where my grandparents ran a general store and I was raised, we are not newcomers to this ridge. A mile away from here, on top of Cole Hill, is the homestead where my Abenaki grandfather and his twelve brothers and sisters were born. A hundred-year-old sugar maple in front of that house on Cole Hill was planted by my grandfather and his younger brother Jack. Even closer to us are the unmarked burial places of Abenakis and Mohawks and Mohicans who came to the high places to bury their dead, giving their spirits a headstart on their journey along the Great Road of stars in the sky. The work I've done to protect these burial places from developers is another of the reasons we ended up here on the southeastern side of Glass Factory Mountain in the Kaydeross Range.

Away from the sounds of roads and the glare of carbon arc streetlights, it is quiet here. Some would say it is peaceful, but that is not the right word. This land throbs with life in every season and at every hour. And the quiet itself is not truly quiet. In the absence of the noise of jets and air conditioners, internal combustion engines and recorded music that blanket our perceptions in most of the human environments of America, ten thousand subtler voices may be heard.

As if in answer to my thought, a great horned owl calls from the pine tree just outside. It stands at the edge of the slope behind our camp that leads down to a pond where my grandfather fished when he was five decades younger than I am now. *Hoo, hoo-oooo, hoo, hoo, hoo,* a deep call that resonates. Across the pond, perhaps a quarter mile to the west, another owl answers. Its *Hoo, hoo-hoo-hoo, hoo-ooo, hooo-ooo* is a bit higher, the sound of a female. Again the male owl repeats his call, but he doesn't just leave it at the call so well-described in the weatherbeaten *Peterson's Field Guide to the Birds* that sits on the window ledge near my desk. As he continues to call and she answers, the two of them add sounds that are a little like those of a barred owl, a *huuurrrluuuul*, then almost a warble, then a bark, a growl, and finally a sound best expressed in some other language much older on this land than English. In Abenaki traditions, some owls, such as the Screech Owl, are called village guardians. Roosting in trees near our wigwams, they called out an alarm when strangers approached through the forest at night. The Great Horned Owl was seen as the greatest of the hunters. Abenaki men would wear a cap with two ears on it like the tufts of feathers on Horned Owl's head, disguising their silhouette so they could creep close to the deer.

Whenever I hear the Great Horned Owl call from so close in the night, a part of me that is related to the small furred or feathered creatures hunted by these owls gives an involuntary shiver. I see, for a moment in my mind's eye, the scatter of crow feathers I found two moons ago at the base of the old beech tree with a long-ago healed arrow-shaped scar upon its trunk that says it was once a marker tree. Something deep in my blood remembers that it, too, may be the hunted, that a human being is neither above nor apart, that the land will swallow me as surely as it has the young crow that stirred from its roosting place in the night to be astonished at a sudden, brief burst of starlight as the owl's wide-open talons struck and then darkness swallowed its vision. And from that moment of mortal awareness I find what may seem to some a strange reassurance. To be a Native of the land means accepting it in all of its incarnations. To flow forever with the land, to continue with its cycles, means being aware of death, to know that it has many voices and that the owl's call may be one of them.

Owls. *Kokohas* is one of the names the owl gave itself in the Abenaki language spoken by some of my ancestors. In so many of our native languages the animals say their own names and we repeat them as best we can. Today, when we do so, it is usually as haltingly as a tourist trying to ask directions in a foreign land by using a phrase book. But a few of us have listened well enough not only to speak to the animals, but to be answered by them.

The Europeans who came to the northeast were often amazed at the way the Abenakis could "mimic" the birds and animals, calling a moose with a horn made from a roll of birchbark, bringing a fox by making the squealing cry of a rabbit in distress, or talking a wary turkey into making itself seen. Vocalizations. So I heard it described when I was a student of Wildlife Conservation at Cornell University, where none of my professors spoke about animals or birds actually speaking. Bird and animal calls (or cries, or, more poetically, songs) weren't true language. Or, if they did speak recognizable human words—as captive crows and starlings have often done—then those dumb creatures were only mimicking real speech. Much like the Abenakis, whose ability to do so well at vocal mimicry of the lower orders was explained as a result of their being closer on the evolutionary ladder to beasts than were Europeans. In fact, in the early days of the European migrations, learned men believed that American Indians were neither fully human nor truly capable of speech. The ringing grace of native oratory was said to be like bird song, beautiful utterance devoid of meaning. When there were no Europeans around to hear them, Indians were said to growl and mumble at each other in the manner of wolves and bears. It is very much an understatement to say that we were not respected. Few Europeans learned our languages. Liked tamed crows, we were expected to speak in their tongues.

The old relationship which my Abenaki people appear to have had with this land, with all that lived upon, within and above it, was and remains for some of us a dialogue. Not a simple one, but one as complex as all of life. Today, American Indians have been elevated (or reduced) to the status of environmental icons, as much in balance with nature as the spider, with its instinctively spun web. It is a perilous balance into which we have been thrust. We become noble savages, whether we like it or not. Then, if we (and all of our ancestors and all of our descendants) do not live up to this, if white researchers can shove enough data onto the page to prove that Indians didn't really act like environmentalists all the time in every situation, we are taken to the other extreme. Rather than respecting the buffalo, such researchers say, the Plains Indians wiped out entire herds indiscriminately—using research like a scapel to cut the cord that bound human beings to the buffalo people like an umbilical. Such researchers conclude that our First Nations didn't wipe out all the buffalo herds simply because our populations were too small, dropping Indians back down to the status that we shared at times in colonial America with the wolf, or the mountain lion—dangerous predators with bounties on our scalps. In American culture iconization is only one step away from exposure and vilification. In American Indian culture, people are not icons; and we humans are never more than one step away from every other part of creation.

It is a dialogue still—speaking with, engaging in a deep relationship, marrying the land. So many of our tradtions bear witness to such intimacy. As I listen to the owls speaking to each other, moving through the forest, engaging in a slow dance over the next three hours that takes them in a great circle around the pond, up slope and down, from the birches to the pines on the high slope, I remember one of our stories. It tells how Great Horned Owl fell in love with a young Penobscot woman who said she would marry only the greatest hunter. So he disguised himself as a human, placing a hood over his head. Then he came into the village, carrying a deer he'd killed over his shoulder. Everyone thought he would make a perfect husband, except for the young woman, who was suspicious of this young man who always kept his head covered. She urged him to sit with her by the fire, moving him closer to it until the heat was so great that he had to take off his hood. As soon as he did his tufted ears stood up high above his head.

"This one is not a human being," the young woman cried out as Great Horned Owl assumed his own shape and flew off. "I cannot marry him."

But Great Horned Owl was persistent, trying again and again to win the young woman. Finally, close to despair, Great Horned Owl stopped trying to imitate a human being. He sat in a tree at the edge of the village and began to play a song on his flute. It was so hauntingly beautiful that the young woman could not help but be moved by it.

She left her lodge and walked into the forest. "I will marry you," she said. Then Great Horned Owl flew down and carried her away.

II. Turkeys
September 11, 2000

The leaves of the blueberry bushes—more than fifty of them planted forty years ago by the people who lived here before selling us what was their much-loved summer camp—are starting to turn red. This wet spring and summer have made the blueberry crop abundant. We've picked all that we can eat or freeze and given just as many berries away. Such abundance is meant to be shared—as the cedar waxwings and chickadees and bluejays who flutter around my head as I pick are well aware. Though I prune out the dead wood, weed and mulch, the birds know these berries are theirs. In fact, last summer, when the harvest was much less than this one, most of the berries were picked by them.

Before I can write another sentence, Carol comes into the room. "Come quick," she says. "The wild turkeys are in the blueberries."

We've put in a new double-glazed picture window and our view of the berry bushes, and the cut through the trees below them, is spectacular. On some days we can see thirty miles southeast—across the hills where the Hudson River winds, invisible most days save as a winding snake of rising mist past Easton, New York, and on to the lower edge of Vermont's Green Mountains. Today, though, the clouds have settled around the hill. Though we can see our yard, the world beyond it turns into ghostly mist past the tall elegance of the white birches.

In the rain-shadowed bushes where I stood barefoot only half an hour ago to pick a pint of berries for our breakfast, one large turkey is barely visible standing still, head up and listening. Then he bobs his head, making the beard on his chest swing back and forth as he walks deeper in among the bushes. Two more are on the driveway, their feathers bronze, iridescent, glittering as if they carry light with them. We often hear them in the woods around us, the scratching of their feet as they forage for insects, seeds and berries, their voices repeating the flock call to each other. *Kee-yow, kee-yow.* "You still there?" *Kee-yow, kee-yow.* "I'm still here. Where are you?"

Here in the Northeast, as the forests have been allowed to reclaim the land that was once cleared, the old ecosystems have begun to reassert themselves. At the turn of the 20th century, white-tail deer had become so rare that people came from miles around when one was killed and hung up in front of the country store in Greenfield Center. On this very ridge there were almost no trees, no deer, no turkeys, only herds of sheep grazing the rock-strewn pastures. But now there are deer everywhere, at times though, a little arrogantly. I keep finding the same perfect hoof mark, remade almost every morning at the edge of the garden where our canna lilies and hosta have been grazed down to the level of mowed grass by a buck, who has finally moved on to our neighbor's garden for the more interesting salad course of pole beans and sunflowers. Two years ago, the people in the house closest to ours had to rescue their dog when it found itself under the hooves of a doe who resented the fact that the dog had gotten too close to her fawn. While Mama danced the macarena on Rover, the fawn stood next to their driveway with one of those innocent "What is this all about?" looks on its face that children sometimes wear when they've gotten someone else into trouble. The dog was on its back, the doe pounding it so determinedly with her hooves that for awhile the deer ignored the fact that our neighbor was hitting her with a broom. (Not a truly wise thing to do, for deer have been known to stand on their hind legs and strike out at people with their sharp hooves.) Even after they rescued the only slightly injured dog and retreated with it into their house, the doe, its ears lowered back against its head, kept walking back and forth in their driveway, making a chuffing sound like a horse and looking to finish off the job she'd started.

The more you know an animal, someone once said, the more human it seems. So it is that researchers in Africa are always anthropomorphizing the chimps or lions or gorillas that they study, and giving them human names. In the old days, however, among our people, it was the opposite. The animals gave us their names and the more our Native ancestors saw and heard of the natural world around us, the more they realized that we humans were part of it. What European cultures called "wilderness," carefully separating it from "civilization," remained an intimate part of human nature in indigenous cultures. Rather than pasting human masks over the faces of the animals, we recognized the animals as people with nations of their own. Though we often hunted them, we also gave them respect. Not only did they provide us with food and material goods, they were always teaching us.

The turkey's loud ululating call was an important signal among our people. Sometimes the warriors used it in those days when they tried to protect the land from the inexorable European tide rolling west and north. Turkey, an Iroquois story says, was a great, brave warrior. Long ago there were giants made of stone, cannibals who ate the people and broke down the forests beneath the feet. One day, Turkey and Moose, another one of the old ones in our Abenaki stories, decided to make war on those monsters. Like those material objects which bore Abenaki names—the tobaggan, the moccasin, the tomahawk—the name by which Moose is known is the one by which we called him. Mos, the one who grazes under the waters of the pond.

First, Turkey and Moose found the deep tracks of the Stone Giants. Even without those footprints, which sank at places into the stone itself, it was easy to follow the monsters, for they left a path a devastation behind them like that made by the whirlwind. Then, Turkey and Moose crept up to the place where the Stone Giants were gathered at the edge of a cliff. Turkey gave his loud war cry and flew at them, pecking at their eyes. Moose lowered his horns and charged at them. Surprised by Turkey's cry, and struck by Moose's horns, the Stone Giants stumbled backwards, fell over the cliff, and were killed. Moose's horns were flattened from striking the Stone Giants. Turkey's throat was stained red by their blood. Then Moose and Turkey each cut the hair from the top of the dead Stone Giants. To this day, Turkey wears that hair on his chest and Moose wears it on his chin, as a badge of courage.

Despite their courage, the turkeys—like the moose—were wiped out from this land. Yet they are back again now. And not only the turkeys. Over the last few decades the moose population of Maine, where a number of those great ungulates survived into the 20th century (though elk and caribou became extinct), has risen. As forests have reclaimed the farm lands, in the form of sumac and cherry, followed by locust and ash and maple, wandering young bulls and cows have also moved back into their old ranges in New Hamshire, Vermont, and here in the Adirondacks. Just beyond the blueberry orchard, among the young pines, we have found moose scat—white cowflop-shaped piles—as well as the tracks of a bull, a cow and a calf.

Our old words keep returning to the land.

III. Turtles

September 12, 2000

We've made a narrow walkway of old planks across the end of Bucket Pond, where its shallow waters give way to hummocks of vegetation, ferns rising up on masses of roots to make small islands colonized by pitcher plants and saplings. This morning, as we crossed, I saw a painted turtle just as it saw us. It turned, its feet churning the dark rotted vegetation which forms the bed of the pond—perfect for African violets, said the man who was disappointed when his offer to buy the pond and dredge it out for greenhouse soil was refused.

As the turtle paddled toward the deeper water of the pond where it could dive down out of sight, I moved without thinking—the fastest way to move through the swamp or the forest. I don't recall leaping off the boardwalk, my feet touching one hummock and then another. I only know that somehow I ended up on my stomach, leaning out over the water as my hand grasped the smooth, strong shell of the turtle. Its long claws pushed back hard against my thumb and fingers. Long claws characterize the male painted turtle. *Chrysemes picta.* I lifted it gently. Its carapace was just a little larger than my palm, as the male turtles are smaller than the females. It extended its neck, trying to push free, the yellow stripes from its mouth,back along its wet neck, glowing almost as if lit from within.

One of our old stories tells how Turtle, long ago, decided to make war on human beings because they were hunting the animals without mercy. So Turtle painted yellow lines upon on his face to show that he was serious about taking the path to war. Great as his plans were, however, Turtle met failure and barely escaped alive, his shell cracked as a result. But, like this small reluctant warrior I held in my hand, even though every painted turtle since still wears these martial colors, today turtles flee from the sight of a human being. It is easy to plan war, they've learned, but fighting is a hard thing to do. Perhaps this little one, after I released it, would reinforce that ancient lesson, telling the other turtles in the pond about its narrow escape.

There are many lessons to be learned from the turtles. On the back of every turtle are thirteen large plates, with twenty-eight smaller ones around the edge. Not just the painted turtle, but other turtles around the world share this physical trait. In the late 1960s I did a three-year stint as a volunteer teacher in West Africa. Near dawn one day, as I drove the newly completed Tema Motorway (its ten mile length then the only stretch of four-lane paved highway in Ghana, West Africa), I saw a familiar rounded shape in the middle of the road. I pulled over to dodge the traffic—brightly painted lorries with such mottos on their sides as SEA NEVER DRY and NO TELEPHONE TO HEAVEN—to rescue an African land tortoise, shocked into immobility by the unexpected roar of trucks in the middle of an ancient migration path. Its movable fortress might discourage a leopard or a baboon, but would offer little protection from the Michelins of a ten-ton lorry. As I carried it far off the road and into the brush I counted the familiar thirteen plates on its carapace and smiled up at the full African moon, still visible low above the horizon.

There are thirteen full moons in any given year, roughly twenty eight days between one full moon and the next. So it is that the native people of the northeast say that the turtle's back is a lunar calendar, its scutes counting off the moons and days. And, just as it holds the moon, the turtle also holds the earth. Not the painted turtle, but its bigger cousin, *Chelydra serpentina,* the snapping turtle. There are snapping turtles in Bucket Pond, too, which is not surprising. The range of the painted turtle and the snapper overlap. Of the reptiles of North America, it seems that only the garter snake has a wider range than the snapping turtle. A great many people seem to not just dislike snapping turtles but to be phobic about them as well. Few people are ever bitten by a snapping turtle—unless they've been teasing one they have taken captive—but the image of snapping turtles swimming up beneath you to take a nip out of whatever tender part of the human anatomy is readily available starts the theme for JAWS churning in the subconscious of most people who hear that these tough ancient survivors are in some body of water.

But it isn't that way for us. American Indians see the snapper in a much more favorable way—though not always to its benefit. I doubt that snapping turtles themselves appreciate how sweet traditional turtle stew tastes and how good turtle shell rattles sound during a social dance. Yet it also means that a pond with snapping turtles has always been seen as a valuable resource. More than one Native person has told me about doing as I've done in late summer, gathering up just-hatched snapping turtle babies digging their way from the warm sand, to carry them down to the safety of a swamp, thereby sparing them the dangerous overland journey where many such hatchlings are carried off by crows and hawks, foxes, raccoons and skunks.

The ridge above the pond where our small camp was built is open to the rays of the morning sun. Just behind the house, the steep, wooded ridge runs down to Bucket Pond. Beneath the tall pines and hemlocks, maples and beech, in the rich humus on the well-drained, rocky slope, ground pine and partridge berry twine around the wide basal leaves of Pink Lady's Slippers (*Cypripedium acaule*)—perhaps the largest of the native North American orchids. They grow here in great abundance. This year, between May and July, when their bright inflated, moccasin-like blossoms bobbed at the end of their leafless stalks, we counted more than a hundred blossoms. Some had even crept into the blueberry orchard. Abundant as they might seem, we've taken care that our trails down to the pond go around them. They vanish quickly—not just when an area is logged, but also when trampled by human feet. Their beauty has also been their undoing in the past when people have dug them up, thinking to transplant them into gardens, where they fail to propagate. Called "moccasin flower" by both the Abenaki and Iroquois, they were respected as medicine plants. Though I know how their root may be used, I neither dig them from the earth nor tell anyone else what sort of medicine can be made from the Lady's Slipper. The medicinal use of native ginseng (*Panax quinnquefolium*), also to be found in secluded locations in our woods, along with its smaller cousin the dwarf ginseng (*Panax trifolium*), was too well-known by Europeans. Prized in the orient as an aphrodisiac and blood stimulant, it has become almost completely extirpated from its original habitat here in the southern Adirondacks.

Because the sandy soil around our camp is open to the sun, it grows warm much sooner than anywhere else on our property. The Pink Moccassin Flowers do not venture out onto this baking earth. But others do—the turtles. Every year, usually when a warm spring rain is falling, we look out of the window to see the rain-glossed shell of one or more female painted turtles, front feet gripping the earth as one back leg scoops a hole deeper and deeper until her backside tilts down into it so she can lay her cache of eggs. Each granular surfaced yellowish-white egg is about the size of the last joint of my index finger. Usually, each female lays no more than six or eight eggs, buried about six inches deep in a hole about the width of two fingers. When she is done, she covers the hole thoroughly, scraping earth and vegetation over it so meticulously that it is hard to see that the excavation was ever made. It is important that such care is taken, to protect the eggs from the skunks and raccoons which nose them out at night. More than once I've gone out in the morning to find only a scraped-out hollow, mute evidence of a midnight snack where a turtle's nest had been.

One such rainy day I watched a single painted turtle for more than two hours on our lawn (if you could use that term for the sandy, unseeded half acre that we gave over to native grasses and plants) and observed that nest camouflage is not a mother turtle's only way of protecting the next generation. After finishing one hole, which took her a good fifteen minutes to dig, she covered it rather carelessly and crawled on without laying a single egg. She dug two more such decoy nests before her final one, close to a clump of milkweed that would later serve as late-summer food for Monarch butterfly caterpillars. That final nest was the one that was the most carefully concealed.

This morning, a particularly warm one, I pay close attention to the small raised garden I made this spring, using old railroad ties to hold in the composted soil made in lasagna layers from grass clippings and cow manure, shredded waste paper and kitchen scraps. A few tomato plants, some beans and onions, carrots and a few rows of snapdragons, zinnias and dinner plate dahlias have done well there this year, though the heavier-than-usual rains doomed one planting after another of usually prolific marigolds. The deer have spared this garden, but this past spring brought quite another, unexpected, peril to the survival of the small plants in the form of a mother snapper who discovered the garden's soft earth was a perfect nest site.

Three months before, I had started to walk down to the pond. Two steps past the garden I did a doubletake. When did someone put that large round stone in among the tomato plants? That large round greenish-gray stone . . . with a head? I turned slowly and crouched to approach my invaded garden on my hands and knees so that I would not startle the female snapping turtle who had chosen that spot for her nest. But I needn't have bothered with caution. She was well-settled in and not about to move. She raised her shell slightly, gave one long hiss like a leaking innertube, and then, territorial rights established, settled back into excavating the foot deep hole beneath the rear of her plastron. Even when I cautiously used a yardstick to measure her shell (roughly 10-1/2 inches across and 12 inches long) she paid no further attention to me.

Fearsome and feared as snapping turtles may be to the average person, they pose no real danger. We, though, present a great deal of danger to them. Migrating snappers often end up crushed on our roadways, and are an easy target for men and boys with .22s who shoot turtles for sport, out of fear, or because they view them as unwanted competitors for fish or ducks. Although snapping turtles sometimes climb out onto logs or banks to bask in the sun, as do our painted turtles, more often than not they engage in aquatic basking. Their heads raised up like a small floating stick, they rest for long periods on the surface with most of their carapace above water. Watching them from the hill above the pond with binoculars, I've sometimes seen two or three engaging in this leisurely behavior, an easy target for anyone with a scoped rifle.

In the past, though no longer so much today, snappers were a favored food item for Native Americans and rural people who knew how good the cooked flesh of a snapping turtle tastes. Though it is not strictly true, I grew up being told by my grandmother that just as chickens have white meat and dark meat, there were at least seven different kinds of meat on a snapping turtle with the tastes of pork, chicken, turkey, beef steak, veal, lamb, and rabbit. Though it has been many years since I've tasted snapping turtle meat, cooked Mohawk style in its own shell, I can state from experience that while the meat has the richness of good beef, it does not have seven flavors. At Akwesasne, the Mohawk reservation at the extreme northern tip of New York, the people no longer eat snapping turtles. It is not that they are gone. Turtles are still found in large numbers in the St. Lawrence River that was turned into a seaway, cutting through the heart of not one but two Canadian/U.S. Mohawk reservations—Akweasane which is divided between New York and Quebec, and Kahnawake, close to Montreal. The problem with the snapping turtles today is that that these turtles, which scavenge the river and take in virtually everything in the food chain, have absorbed immense amounts of PCBs and other toxins.

My friend Ward Stone, a wildlife biologist whose sometimes controversial work for New York State has included studying these levels of toxicity, is amazed at how the turtles have survived despite it all, though many of them have cancers on their bodies. Even when cooked, their meat still contains enough heavy metals and PCBs to endanger the health of those who might eat them. Tom Porter, a Mohawk elder who no longer lives at Akwesasne, remembers the day when his family took their fishing nets and laid them on the banks of the St. Lawrence, leaving them there to return to the earth, as the fish and other river creatures were no longer safe to eat. The aluminum plants of Reynolds and Kaiser continue to pour their wastes into the air and river to this day, making the Akwesasne Mohawk Reservation—an American Indian superfund site—one of the most chemically poisoned places in North America.

The snapper was also sought by the Iroquois and other nations of the Northeast to use its shell in the making of rattles, with the dried outstretched neck used as the handle (braced by two thin ash withes fastened along the back of its neck from the shell to beyond the tip of its nose). Such rattles are made to this day. I have one hanging over our fireplace here at the camp, its shell dimensions just an inch or two less than my garden turtle. It was given to me seven years ago while I was in Wisconsin by Pam Green, an Oneida Indian poet. It was made by her traditionalist husband who wanted to thank me for doing storytelling for the teachers and students of the Oneida Indian School. Such a gift is a great honor, not only because of the care required to make such a rattle, but because of the place those rattles hold in our Northeastern cultures. Not only do they provide the rhythm for social and ceremonial dances, they are made from the body of one of the most revered of all beings. To the Iroquois, the snapping turtle is a powerful and sacred creature. It is not just a creature of one element, but travels between both the earth and the water—just as one who is a medicine person is able to travel between the human world and that of the spirits.

But to the Iroquois and perhaps a hundred different American Indian tribal nations all across this continent, the turtle also plays another role which makes it the greatest of all the beings that walk and swim. Long ago, the stories say, there was no earth. Everything was covered with water. For some reason, the water beings decided that earth needed to be created. Each Native tradition may differ slightly here. Some, like the Iroquois, tell of a woman who fell from the land above the sky. Seeing her fall, the geese flew up to catch her and the water creatures began to make a place for her to stand. One thing is common to every version of that story, which is called the "Earth Diver motif" by folklorists. Someone had to dive down below the waters to bring up some mud to make the solid land of Earth. But when it was brought up, where could it be placed? One being volunteered. Floating upon the surface just as an aquatic basking snapper would to this day, Great Snapping Turtle said that the new earth could be placed upon his back. There, the mud was placed there and as it was smoothed and spread out it grew to be the continent of North America—the land that the majority of contemporary American Indians often refer to as Turtle Island.

That June morning, the mother snapping turtle remained splayed in position between my staked tomato plants, slowly laying her eggs. In a half hour she laid more than two dozen of them. Each egg was as white and round as a ping-pong ball, though just a bit smaller. As she laid each egg she squeezed shut her eyes—each pupil like a starburst—and there was moisture at the edge of each eye. Though not as dramatically as do the sea turtles while laying, the mother snapping turtle cried as she laid her eggs. At last, almost carelessly, she pulled the edge of her shell up out of the hole and shoved back enough earth to cover the eggs. Then she levered herself out of the garden, dragging herself with her strong front paws up and over the rail tie wall—which had been no impediment to her powerful nesting urge (and her ability to do this simple equation: soft earth = easy digging)—to make her ponderous way back to the pond. Behind her was left a perfect turtle-shaped imprint. Her haste to depart had little to do with the fact that I was watching. Unlike the painted turtle, snappers cover their nests rather carelessly. And even more than the painted turtle, snapping turtle eggs end up on the menu of raccoons and skunks.

I looked at my raised garden a little ruefully. There was now one fewer pepper plant and a few slightly mangled marigolds, but she had done surprisingly little damage. One turtle, however, was enough. I spent the next hour putting up wire fencing around the garden. It would serve two purposes. Not only would it keep out other mother turtles with a yen for an easy nest site, it would protect that precious clutch of eggs through July and August until the warmth of the late summer sun had finally done its job.

Now September is here. Hatching time. It had been a cool spring and summer. Research has shown that cooler temperatures, around the mid-50s fahrenheit at critical times in the incubation of turtle eggs, result in all the hatchlings being female. Males like it hotter, up in the 70s.

New as that finding may be to western science, I was told over twenty years ago by a Mohawk friend just that same thing. "Cool summer, turtle eggs will be mommas." But that was just Indian folk belief and thus (though as accurate as a vast number of our "folk beliefs" are) scientifically unreliable.

Once again, though, I miss the hatching. When I come back to the camp one evening I can see that the soft earth has been disturbed. When the hatching begins, most seem to come out within a matter of hours. I look around, but see no sign of any little turtles. It is unlikely I would, for they head quickly for shelter, hiding under the leaves when they are tired, making their way toward the pond. Not unerringly, I have to say. On occasion I've found disgruntled baby turtles in our garage, which is downslope in the opposite direction of the pond. Finally, I dig down carefully with my fingers where the nest had been. I find a few small, slightly rubbery, collapsed shells, pushed open from within. Another generation has emerged to take its place, holding up our Mother Earth.

FOR THE LITTLE PEOPLE

On a warm summer day twenty-five years ago I sat outside the Mohegan Indian Museum in Uncasville, Connecticut with Gladys Tantaquidgeon. I'd just spent the morning with her, guided through the museum that she and her brother Harold founded, not only to preserve the material culture of their often-overlooked people, but also to keep alive something more subtle and more enduring—the Mohegan spirit. It was decades before the Indian casinos of Connecticut would once again put the tribal nations along the Thames into the headlines, prompting articles on the one hand that heralded the revival of the Mohegans and Pequots or, on the other hand, attacked them as phonies playing Indian for a fast buck. That day, though, there was nothing at stake other than a few hours of conversation and the chance to listen to an elder whose amazing life had already spanned more than seven decades, taking her across America as a student of ethnology and a federal employee working with other Native peoples before returning to Mohegan Hill.

Maybe being raised by my own grandparents has made me cherish such times with elders, made me listen especially close whenever someone with gray hair begins to speak. It is often said among our New England tribal nations that white hair is a badge of honor, an indicator of wisdom, a visible sign that this is one to whom we should listen. When your hair is dark, I've been told, it is your time to travel around and listen. When it grows white, then like the snow settling upon the land, it is your role to remain in place and let those who wish to listen come to you. (Since my own hair—thanks to a dominant European gene for male pattern baldness—seems to be emulating the leaves of autumn rather than the snows of yesteryear, it appears that I may be doomed to a life of perpetual peregrination.)

Maybe, too, my eagerness to hear the words of elders is because a part of me is still that little boy whose bedroom was next to that of his grandparents. I knew they were very old and I was afraid they would die and leave me. Through the open connecting door, I could hear their breathing at night. I would lay awake, listening, listening, and praying that their breath would not stop. I hadn't yet learned that those who die, whose spirits travel to the top of Wonbi Wadzoak (the Great White Mountain now named Mount Washington) and then step up into the sky to walk the Road of Stars (the Milky Way), are never really gone. They return to us in dreams, their voices come to us on the wind and they are no further away than the other side of a leaf that has fallen. Sometimes, too, some part of them returns to us in the next generation, when a reincarnated part of that elder we thought was lost forever, is restored to us by a boy or girl—a son or daughter of our own whose looks and gestures and ways of living are so like those of the departed that we know whose eyes look out at us from that young face.

In any event, if on that summer day a part of me was worrying that Gladys Tantaquidgeon would not be around much longer, such anxiety was uncalled for. In the year 2000, Gladys Tantaquidgeon celebrated her 101st birthday. And, on that day, in her seventies, she was more alive and lively than most thirty-year-olds. There were many things discussed that day, but the one small thing that stuck with me most was little more than a shared gesture and a smile. At exactly the same moment, just before we began to eat, each of us tore a small piece off our sandwiches and leaned over to place it on the earth. Our eyes met and Gladys smiled.

"Oh," she said, "you do that, too?"

I nodded.

Her small smile grew just a little broader. "For the Little People," she said as we both placed our offerings beneath the branches of a small bush.

For the Little People. At this point I might observe that a widespread belief in the Little People, often described as "Little Indians dressed in old-time clothes," is one of the most enduring cultural artifacts of the New England tribes. But I prefer to say it another way—that respect for these Little People continues to this day, as do regular sightings and numerous actual encounters with them among the Native peoples of Ndakinna (as we call it in Abenaki, a word simply meaning

"Our Land"). Wherever I have traveled in Native New England I've been given stories about the little ones—often first-person accounts.

Not everyone, however, who shares a story about a human encounter with the Little People will admit that they were the person who experienced it. This usually isn't to escape ridicule—unless they're telling the tale to a non-Indian. Certain kinds of encounters with the Little People are said to bring good fortune, especially if the Little Person is not surprised by the human, but allows himself or herself to be seen. However, the Little People listen to us as much as we look for them. If they hear a human bragging about seeing one, they'll make sure never to show themselves to that loose-lipped person again!

Twenty years ago, I was visiting Steve Laurent and his wife Margie in Intervale, New Hampshire, at their small Abenaki Indian Shop on the small piece of land where members of the Laurent family have engaged in the tourist trade for so long that the place has earned a historical landmark designation and a planned by-pass road ten years ago was rerouted to go around them. (More about roads and Little People later.)

As I wandered through the shop, Margie looked over at Steve. I don't recall what I had just said or done, but a small nod passed between them. Perhaps they knew I was ready to listen. Or perhaps they felt that I needed to be cautioned, to hear the lesson that the story they were about to share with me contained. Listen close when a Native elder tells you a story. The lesson within it may be a subtle way of suggesting to you that you need to rethink your behavior.

"There was a man," Margie said, taking me gently by the arm, "who wanted to see the Manongimasak, the Little People. There was this place by the river where everyone knew that the Little People came at night. They would see shapes of clay left on the banks from the Little People making their pots. People told that man that the Little People didn't like to be bothered, but he was determined. He took his canoe to that place and turned it upside down and left it there for a few nights. Then, when he felt that the Little People had gotten used to it, he went there before dark and got underneath his canoe to hide.

"The next day everyone was waiting for him to come back to the village. But the morning passed and he didn't return. All that day he didn't come back. When it got to be night, some people thought maybe the man liked seeing them so much that he was waiting around for the next show. But on the morning of the second day they got worried.

"A group of people went to that place. There was the man's canoe, not upside down but rightside up. The man was nowhere to be seen, but there was a pile of clay on the riverbank. It was about two feet tall and a little longer than a man. There was a little hole where the mouth would be, and when they leaned close they could hear someone saying help in a weak voice. When they broke open that clay, there was the man who had wanted to see the Little People. He was so weak and scared that he couldn't say anything, but when he finally recovered he told them his story. He'd been waiting and waiting for the Little People to arrive. Just when he thought they weren't going to show up he began to hear voices whispering all around him. Then, all of a sudden, the canoe was rolled off of him and the last thing he remembered was lots of little hands grabbing him.

"That man never tried to see the Little People again."

While attending the Passamaquoddy Ceremonial Days in the early '80s, I heard yet another story about an unpleasant experience of seeing the Little People. The state was planning to build a road through a part of the reservation where the Little People were known to live. Such places, often areas with prominent rockfaces, cliffs or small valleys, have been described as the home to one particular sort of Little People by not just my Algonquin-speaking relatives, but by our Iroquois neighbors to the west. The Iroquois, who call the Little People *Jo-ge-oh* (or, at Akwesasne, Jungies) say that there are different tribes among them. Some have the responsibility of caring for the plants, watering them with dew carried in cups made of flowers. Those who live among the cliffs defend their territory fiercely and are referred to as Rock Throwers.

To prepare for the new road, which the Pleasant Point Passamaquoddys did not want, a crew of surveyors came to the reservation to mark the right-of-way. A few hours after leaving to start work they came running back into town, bloody and bruised. They said a gang of little Indian kids wearing old time clothing had attacked them with stones while they were trying to survey that rockface. The stones, thrown hard and with great accuracy, had broken their surveying instruments, and they had to run for their lives.

"Those weren't our kids," the Passamaquoddys told them. "Our kids are all in school today."

The surveyors left Pleasant Point and the road was never built.

One of the tribes of Little People live underwater. Their faces, it is said, are as thin and sharp as the blade of a hatchet. When someone sees them paddling one of their canoes on the surface of a river or lake, they usually sink out of sight. Those canoes of the Little People are pretty versatile, I might add. They can act like a submarine or go through the air. Mdawelasis, an Abenaki elder, lived for many years in Old Forge, New York where he worked in a tourist attraction called the Enchanted Forest. One day as we worked on carving a cedar pole in his backyard he told me that he had once heard singing coming first from the direction of the Moose River and then from overhead. He looked up just in time to see a small canoe with little Indians in it paddling across the sky.

The Abenakis at Odanak, the refugee community east of Montreal where New England native people from many different tribes ended up during the dislocations of the eighteenth and nineteenth centuries, say that the Little People lived in the St. Francis River by their village. If any enemies came upstream to attack the village, the underwater Little People, who were the friends of the Abenakis, would tip over the enemy canoes and drown the would-be attackers. Rick Obomsawin, an Odanak Abenaki, told me that in recent years it was thought that the Little People of the river were no longer there. But in 1998, while canoeing with my younger son Jesse who was staying at Odanak to increase his fluency in speaking Abenaki, they found something by the river that filled Rick with delight. On a certain bank were many little shapes in clay that looked like wheels, a sign that the Little People had recently been there making pots.

While at the wedding of an Abenaki friend near Pawlet, Vermont, I was told another story of the underwater Little People by Molly Keating, another Abenaki who had worked for years to preserve our culture and build alliances among our various New England Native peoples. Her father, she told me, was once out canoeing with a friend. They came around a sharp bend in the river and there, right in front of them, was a tiny canoe with three Little People in it. They were so close that her father could hear what they were saying.

"Turn around and greet the Big People," said the Little Person in the back of the canoe.

"No," said the one in the front. "You greet them."

"That's right," said the one in the middle. "You should greet them because you are the best-looking one of us all."

Then, Molly's father told her, the Little Person in the back did just that. He turned around and grinned at them. "And he was really ugly!" Molly's father added. Then the canoe and its three small paddlers sank out of sight.

Perhaps the best way for me to sink out of sight, to conclude this piece that is more memoir than scholarly consideration, is with these two questions that I know some of my readers may be asking by now. Do I believe in the Little People? I certainly do. Have I ever had an encounter of my own with them? Well, that's a good question.

THE SNAPPING TURTLE

My grandmother was working in the flower garden near the road that morning when I came out with my fishing pole. She was separating out the roots of iris. As far as flowers go, she and I were agreed that iris had the sweetest scent. Iris would grow about anywhere, shooting up green sword-shaped leaves like the mythical soldiers that sprang from the planted teeth of a dragon. But iris needed some amount of care. Their roots would multiply so thick and fast that they could crowd themselves right up out of the soil. Spring separating and replanting were, as my grandmother put it, just the ticket.

(Later that day, I knew, she would climb into our blue 1951 Plymouth to drive around the back roads of Greenfield, a box of iris in the back seat. She would stop at farms where she had noticed a certain color of iris that she didn't have yet. Up to the door she would go to ask for a root so that she could add another splash of color to our garden. And, in exchange, she would give that person, most often a flowered-aproned and somewhat elderly woman like herself, some of her own iris.

It wasn't just that she wanted more flowers herself. She had a philosophy. If only one person kept a plant, something might happen to it. Early frost, insects, animals, Lord knows what. But if many had that kind of plant, then it might survive. Sharing meant a kind of immortality. I didn't quite understand it then, but I enjoyed taking those rides with her, carrying boxes and cans and flowerpots with new kinds of iris back to the car.)

"Going fishing, Sonny?" she said.

Of course, she knew where I was going. Not only the evidence of the pole in my hand, but also the simple fact that it was a Saturday morning in late May and I was a boy of ten, would have led her to that natural conclusion. But she had to ask. It was part of our routine.

"Un-hun," I answered, as I always did. "Unless you and Grampa need some help." Then I held my breath, for though my offer of aid had been sincere enough, I really wanted to go fishing.

Grama thrust her foot down on the spading fork, carefully levering out a heavy clump of iris marked last fall with a purple ribbon to indicate the color. She did such things with half my effort and twice the skill, despite the fact I was growing, as she put it, like a weed. "No, you go on along. This afternoon Grampa and I could use some help, though."

"I'll be back by then," I said, but I didn't turn and walk away. I waited for the next thing I knew she would say.

"You stay off of the state road, now."

In my grandmother's mind, Route 9N, which came down the hill past my grandparents' little gas station and general store on the corner, was nothing less than a Road of Death. If I ever set foot on it, I would surely be as doomed as our four cats and two dogs that met their fates there.

"Runned over and kilt," as Grampa Jess put it.

Grampa Jesse, who had been the hired man for my grandmother's parents before he and Grama eloped, was not a person with booklearning like my college-educated grandmother. His family was Abenaki Indian, poor but honest hill people who could read the signs in the forest, but who had never traipsed far along the trails of schoolhouse ways. Between Grama's books and Grampa's practical knowledge, some of which I was about to apply to bring home a mess of trout, I figured I was getting about the best education a ten-year-old boy could have. I was lucky that my grandparents were raising me.

"I'll stay off the state road," I promised. "I'll just follow Bell Brook."

Truth be told, the state road made me a little nervous, too. It was all too easy to imagine myself in the place of one of my defunct pets, stunned by the elephant bellow of a tractor-trailer's horn, looking wild-eyed up to the shiny metal grill. Then the thud, the lightning-bolt flash of light, and eternal dark. I imagined my grandfather shoveling the dirt over me in a backyard grave next to that of Lady, the collie, and Kitty-kitty, the gray cat, while my grandmother dried her eyes with her apron and said, "I told him to stay off that road!"

I was big on knowledge but very short on courage in those years. I mostly played by myself because the other kids my age from the houses and farms scattered around our rural township regarded me as a Grama's boy who would tell if they were to tie me up and threaten to burn my toes with matches, a ritual required to join the local society of pre-teenage boys. A squealer. And they were right.

I didn't much miss the company of other kids. I had discovered that most of them had little interest in the living things around them. They were noisier than Grampa and I were, scaring away the rabbits that we could creep right up on. Instead of watching the frogs catching flies with their long, gummy tongues, those boys wanted to shoot them with their BB guns. I couldn't imagine any of them having the patience or inclination to hold out a hand filled with sunflower seeds, as Grampa had showed me I could, long enough for a chickadee to come and land on an index finger.

Even fishing was done different when I did it Grampa's way. I knew for a fact that most of those boys would go out and come home with an empty creel. They hadn't been watching for fish from the banks as I had in the weeks before the trout season began, so they didn't know where the fish lived. They didn't know how to keep low, float your line in, wait for that first tap, and then, after the strike that bent your pole, set the hook. And they never said thank you to every fish they caught, the way I remembered to do.

Walking the creek edge, I set off downstream. By mid-morning my bait can of moss and red earthworms that Grampa and I had dug from the edge of our manure pile was near empty. I'd gone half a mile and already caught seven trout. All of them were squaretails, native brook trout whose sides were patterned with a speckled rainbow of bright circles— red, green, gold. I'd only kept the ones more than seven inches long, and I'd remembered to wet my hand before taking the little ones off the hook. Grasping a trout with a dry hand would abrade the slick coat of natural oil from the skin and leave it open for infection and disease.

As always, I'd had to keep the eyes in the back of my head open just as Grampa had told me to do whenever I was in the woods. "Things is always hunting one another," he'd said.

And he was right. Twice, at places where Bell Brook swung near Mill Road, I'd had to leave the stream banks to take shelter when I heard the ominous crunch of bicycle tires on gravel. Back then, when I was ten, I was smaller than the other boys my age. I made up for it by being harder to catch. Equal parts of craftiness, and plain old panic at being collared by bullies I viewed as close kin to Attilla the Hun, kept me slipperier than an eel.

From grapevine tangles up the bank, I'd watched as Pauly Roffmeier, Ricky Holstead, and Will Backus rolled up to the creek, making more noise than a herd of hippos, to plunk their own lines in. Both times, they caught nothing. It wasn't surprising, since they were talking like jaybirds, scaring away whatever fish might have been within half a mile. And Will kept lighting matches and throwing them down to watch them hiss out when they struck the water. Not to mention the fact that I had pulled a ten-inch brook trout out of the first hole and an eleven incher out of the second before they even reached the stream.

I looked up at the sky. I didn't wear a watch then. No watch made by man seemed able to work more than a few days when strapped to my wrist. It was a common thing on my Grampa's side of the family. "We jest got too much 'lectricity in us," he explained.

Without a watch, I could measure time by the sun. I could see it was about ten. I had reached the place where Bell Brook crossed under the state road. Usually I went no further than this. It had been my boundary for years. But somewhere along the way I had decided that day would be different. I think perhaps a part of me was ashamed of hiding from the other boys, ashamed of being always afraid. I wanted to do something that I'd always been afraid to do. I wanted to be brave.

I had no need to fish further. I had plenty of trout for our supper. I'd cleaned them all out with my Swiss Army knife, leaving the entrails where the crows and jays could get them. If you did that, the crows and jays would know you for a friend and not sound the alarm when they saw you walking in the woods. I sank the creel under water and wedged it beneath a stone. The water of the brook was deep and cold and I knew it would keep the flesh of the trout fresh and firm. Then I cached my pole and bait can under the spice bushes. As I looked up at the highway, Grama's words came back to me:

"Stay off the state road, Sonny."

"*Under*," I said aloud, "*is* not *on*."

Then, taking a deep breath, bent over at the waist, I waded into the culvert that dove under the Road of Death. I had gone no more than half a dozen steps before I walked into a spider web so strong that it actually bounced me back. I splashed a little water from the creek up onto it and watched the beads shape a pattern of concentric circles. The orb-weaver sat unmoving in a corner, one leg resting on a strand of the web. She'd been waiting for the vibration of some flying creature caught in the sticky strands of her net. Clearly, I was much more than she had hoped for. Her wide back was patterned with a shape like that of a red and gold hourglass. Her compound eyes, jet black on her head, took in my giant shape. Spiders gave some people the willies. I knew their bite would hurt like blue blazes, but I still thought them graced with great beauty.

"Excuse me," I said. "Didn't mean to bother you."

The spider raised one front leg. A nervous reaction, most likely, but I raised one hand back. Then I ducked carefully beneath the web, entering an area where the light was different. It was like passing from one world into another. I sloshed through the dark culvert, my fingertips brushing the rushing surface of the stream, the current pushing at my calves. My sneakered feet barely held their purchase on the ridged metal, slick with moss.

When I came out the other side, the sunlight was blinding. Just ahead of me the creek was overarched with willows. They were so thick and low that there was no way I could pass without either going underwater or breaking a way through the brush. I wasn't ready to do either. So I made my way up the bank, thinking to circle back and pick up the creek further down, for what purpose, I wasn't sure, aside from just wanting to do it. I was nervous as a hen yard when a chicken hawk is circling overhead. But I was excited, too. This was new ground to me, almost a mile from home. I'd gone farther from home in the familiar directions of north and west, into the safety of the woods, but this was different: across the state road, in the direction of town. Someone else's hunting territory. I stayed low to the ground and hugged the edges of the brush as I moved. Then I saw something that drew me away from the creek—the glint of a wider expanse of water. The Rez. The old Greenfield Reservoir.

I'd never been to the Rez, though I knew the other boys went there. As I'd sat alone on the bus, my bookbag clasped tightly to my chest, I'd heard them talk about swimming there, fishing for bass, spearing bullfrogs five times as big as the little frogs in Bell Brook.

I knew I shouldn't be there, yet I was. Slowly I moved to the side of the wide trail that led to the edge of the deep water, and it was just as well that I did; their bikes had been stashed in the brush down the other side of the path. They'd been more quiet than usual. I might have walked up on them if I hadn't heard a voice.

"Gimme a drag," a voice said, just over the edge of the bank. I slid back, my heart pounding so hard that I knew it sounded like a drum solo.

"You let it go out, jerk," answered another voice that I could barely hear over my deafening heartbeat.

"I'll light it."

I'll light it. Not, *There he is. Let's kill him?* I hadn't been heard or seen. I was still safe. But I was as curious as I was afraid. What were they doing? I had to see.

I picked up some of the dark mud with my finger tips and drew lines across my cheeks. Grampa had explained this would make me harder to be seen. Then I slid to a place where an old tree leaned over the bank, cloaked by the cattails that grew from the edge of the Rez. I made my way out on it and looked. What I saw shocked me. Pauly and Ricky and Will were worse boys than I'd thought. They were really bad! They had a cigarette and they were smoking it.

"Gimme," Ricky said again. "I'm the one who brought it."

"Stole it from your Mommy's handbag, you mean." Pauly held Ricky at arm's length as he puffed and then coughed. "An whyn't you get more than one?"

"If I stole a fresh pack, she would of known for sure. Gimme! I'm the one's gonna be in Dutch if she finds out."

No, I thought. *You're wrong. All of you are going to get in trouble after I tell Grama what I've seen and she gets through calling all your parents.*

As I watched, they shared the cigarette, alternately puffing at it, coughing, dropping it, and relighting it. Finally, when Ricky had puffed down to the filter, the last to get it, their smoking orgy was over. Ricky flicked the butt into the Rez and stared out at the water. "It's not gonna come up," Ricky said. He picked up something that looked like a makeshift spear. "You lied."

"I did not. It was over there. The biggest snapper I ever saw." Will shaded his eyes with one hand and looked right in my direction without seeing me. "If we catch it, we could sell it for ten dollars to that colored man on Congress Street. They say snapping turtles have seven different kinds of meat in them."

"Crap," Pauly said, throwing his own spear aside. "Let's go find something else to do."

One by one, they picked up their fishing poles and went back down the path. I waited without moving, hearing their heavy feet on the trail and then the rattle of their bike chains. I was no longer thinking about going home to tell Grama about their smoking. All I could think of was that snapping turtle.

I knew a lot about turtles. There were mud turtles and map turtles. There was the smart orange-legged wood turtle and the red-eared slider with its cheeks painted crimson as if going to war. Every spring Grama and Grampa and I would drive around, picking up those whose old migration routes had been cut by the recent but lethal ribbons of road. Spooked by a car, a turtle falls into that old defense of pulling head and legs and tail into its once impregnable fortress. But a shell does little good against the wheels of a Nash or a DeSoto.

Some days we'd rescue as many as a dozen, taking them home for a few days before releasing them back into the wild. Painted turtles, several as big as two hands held together, might nip at you some, but they weren't really dangerous. And the wood turtles would learn in a day or so to reach out for a strawberry or a piece of juicy tomato and then leave their heads out for a scratch while you stroked them with a finger.

Snappers, though, they were different. Long-tailed, heavy-bodied and short-tempered, their jaws would gape wide and they'd hiss when you came up on them ashore. Their heads and legs were too big to pull into their shells, so they would heave up on their legs and lunge forward as they snapped at you. They might weigh as much as fifty pounds, and it was said they could take off a handful of fingers in one bite. There wasn't much to recommend a snapping turtle as a friend.

Most people seemed to hate snappers. Snappers ate the fish and the ducks, and scared swimmers away. Or I should say that people hated them alive. Dead, they were supposed to be the best-eating turtle of all. *Ten dollars*, I thought. *Enough for me to send away to the mail-order pet place and get a pair of real flying squirrels.* I'd kept the clipping from *Field and Stream* magazine thumbtacked over my bed for four months now. A sort of plan was coming into my mind.

People were afraid of getting bit by snappers when they were swimming. But from what I'd read, and from what Grampa had told me, there really wasn't much to worry about.

"Snapper won't bother you none in the water," Grampa said. If you were even to step on a snapping turtle resting on the bottom of a pond, all it would do would be to move away. And on land, all the danger from a snapper came from the front or the side. From behind, a snapper couldn't get you. Get it by the tail, and you were safe. That was the way. And as I thought I kept watch. And as I kept watch I kept up a silent chant inside my mind.

Come here, I'm waiting for you.
Come here, I'm waiting for you.

Before long, a smallish log that had been sticking up farther out in the pond began to drift my way. It was, as I had expected, no log at all. It was a turtle's head. I stayed still. The sun's heat beat on my back, but I lay there like a basking lizard. Closer and closer the turtle came, heading right into water less than waist deep. It was going right for shore, for the sandy bank bathed in sun. I didn't think about why then. I just wondered at the way my wanting seemed to have called it to me.

When it was almost to shore, I slid into the water on the other side of the log. The turtle surely sensed me, for it started to swing around as I stepped slowly toward it, swimming as much as walking. But I lunged and grabbed it by the tail. Its tail was rough and ridged, as easy to hold as if coated with sandpaper. I pulled hard and the turtle came toward me. I stepped back, trying not to fall and pull it on top of me. My feet found the bank and I leaned hard to drag the turtle out, its clawed feet digging into the dirt as it tried to get away. A roaring hiss like the rush of air from a punctured tire came out of its mouth and I stumbled, almost losing my grasp. Then I took another step, heaved again, and it was mine.

Or at least it was until I let go. I knew I could not let go. I looked around, holding its tail, moving my feet to keep it from walking its front legs around to where it would snap at me. It felt as if it weighed a thousand pounds. I could only lift up the back half of its body. I started dragging it toward the creek, fifty yards away. It seemed to take hours, a kind of dance between me and the great turtle, but I did it. I pulled it back through the roaring culvert, water gushing over its shell, under the spider web and past my hidden pole and creel. I could come back later for the fish. Now there was only room in the world for Bell Brook, the turtle, and me.

The long passage upstream is a blur in my memory. I thought of salmon leaping over falls and learned a little that day about how hard such a journey must feel. When I rounded the last bend and reached the place where the brook edged our property, I breathed a great sigh. But I could not rest. There was still a field and the back yard to cross.

My grandparents saw me coming. From the height of the sun it was now midafternoon, and I knew I was dreadful late.

"Sonny, where have you. . .?" began Grama.

Then she saw the turtle.

"I'm sorry. It took so long because of. . ." I didn't finish the sentence because the snapping turtle, undaunted by his backward passage, took that opportunity to try once more to swing around and get me. I had to make three quick steps in a circle, heaving at its tail as I did so.

"Nice size turtle," Grampa Jesse said.

My grandmother looked at me. I realized then I must have been a sight. Wet, muddy, face and hands scratched from the brush that overhung the creek.

"I caught it at the reservoir," I said. I didn't think to lie to them about where I'd been. I waited for my grandmother to scold me. But she didn't.

"Jesse," she said, "Get the big washtub."

My grandfather did as she said. He brought it back and then stepped next to me.

"Leave go," he said.

My hands had a life of their own, grimly determined to never let loose of that all-too-familiar tail, but I forced them to open. The turtle flopped down. Before it could move, my grandfather dropped the big washtub over it. All was silent for a minute as I stood there, my arms aching as they hung by my side. Then the wash tub began to move. My grandmother sat down on it and it stopped.

She looked at me. So did Grampa. It was wonderful how they could focus their attention on me in a way that made me feel as though they were ready to do whatever they could to help.

"What now?" Grama said.

"I heard that somebody down on Congress Street would pay ten dollars for a snapping turtle."

"Jack's," Grampa said.

My grandmother nodded. "Well," she said, "if you go now you

can be back in time for supper. I thought we were having trout." She raised an eyebrow at me.

"I left them this side of the culvert by 9N," I said. "Along with my pole."

"You clean up and put on dry clothes. Your grandfather will get the fish."

"But I hid them."

My grandmother smiled. "Your grandfather will find them." Which he did.

An hour later, we were on the way to Congress Street, the heart of the colored section of Saratoga Springs. In the 1950s Congress Street was like a piece of Harlem dropped into an upstate town. We pulled up in front of Jack's, and a man who looked to be my grandfather's age got up and walked over to us. His skin was only a little darker than my grandfather's, and the two nodded to each other.

My grandfather put his hand on the trunk of the Plymouth.

"What you got there?" Jack said.

"Show him, Sonny."

I opened the trunk. My snapping turtle lifted up its head as I did so.

"I heard you might want to buy a turtle like this for ten dollars," I said.

Jack shook his head. "Ten dollars for a little one like that? I'd give you two dollars."

I looked at my turtle. Had it shrunk in size since Grampa wrestled it into the trunk?

"That's not enough," I said.

"Three dollars. My last offer."

I looked at Grampa. He shrugged his shoulders.

"I guess I don't want to sell it," I said.

"All right," Jack said. "You change your mind, come on back." He touched his hat with two fingers and walked back over to his chair in the sun.

As we drove back toward home, neither of us said anything for awhile. Then my grandfather spoke.

"Would five dollars of been enough?"

"No," I said.

"How about ten?"

I thought about that. "I guess not."

"Why you suppose that turtle was heading for that sandbank?" Grampa said.

I thought about that, too. Then I realized the truth of it.

"It was coming out to lay its eggs."

"Might be."

I thought hard then. I'd learned it was never right for a hunter to shoot a mother animal, as it hurt the next generation to come. Was a turtle any different?

"Can we take her back?" I asked.

"Up to you, Sonny."

And so we did. Gramp drove the Plymouth right up the trail to the edge of the Rez. He held a stick so the turtle would grab onto it as I hauled her out of the trunk. I put her down and she just stayed there, her nose a foot from the water but not moving.

"We'll leave her," Grampa said. We turned to get into the car. When I looked back over my shoulder, she was gone. Only ripples on the water, widening circles rolling on toward other shores, like generations following each other, like my grandmother's flowers still growing in a hundred gardens in Greenfield, like the turtles still seeking out that sandbank, like this story that is no longer just my own but belongs now to your memory, too.

TICKLING A TROUT

Potash isn't a big mountain. On the topo map, showing the Lower Adirondacks near Lake Luzerne, it's listed at 2100 feet. But the way it rises vertically, like a granite plug pushed up from the earth, makes it spectacularly visible from the road as you drive out of town. The view from the top makes the steep half hour scramble up its side more than worthwhile.

That summer day, as a locust in a nearby maple droned a whining song sharp enough to cut through stone, we parked our cars near the stream, at the base of the mountain, to do just that. There were nine of us. My wife Carol, our two small sons, Jim and Jesse, and I had led the way in the old high-finned yellow Plymouth that had been my grandfather's. My sister Mary Ann, her husband Jack, and their children Margo and Zach had followed us in their VW bus. My sister Marge, home for a visit from her job running a health food bakery in Ann Arbor, had ridden with them.

We climbed the mountain, but that isn't what this story is about. Instead, it has to do with what happened when we got out of our cars and started onto the trail by the cold water brook that flowed along the mountain slope. My eyes caught the flash of a square tail in the ripple just before it disappeared from sight.

"There's a trout there," I said. Everyone looked, a little too late.

"No, there's not," said my sister Mary Ann. Only three words, but they invoked the old rivalry that had been set up in our childhood. I'd been raised by my Grandmother and Grandfather, only half a mile from the house where my two younger sisters lived with my parents. Marge was ten years younger than Mary Ann, too young to be part of the competition which included constant and careful comparison of report cards to see who was the better student—until I hit eighth grade and opted out of it by deliberately doing worse in my classes, allowing Mary Ann that edge she so desired.

My two sons looked up at me. I didn't want to argue, but there had been a trout. I answered in a neutral a tone as I could. "There is," I said. "It's a brook trout, about a fourteen incher. It's under that flat rock there." Mary Ann laughed. "There is not a fourteen inch trout there," she said. "You don't know that."

I sat down, took off my T-shirt, my shoes and socks. Then I waded in and walked slowly to the flat rock. Moving my hands with the flow of the current, a finger's width at a time, I slid them palms up under the stone, along the gravely bottom, until I felt the fanning movement of the trout's fins and the silk smoothness of its belly. It wasn't just the slow movement of my hands that was important. Grampa Jesse had taught me that it was what I had in my mind, what I was thinking that counted. No hurry about it. No greed. No anger. Just being calm. Asking the fish to trust you, to give itself to you in a way that was as much a song as it was a wish.

I slid my hands out from beneath the stone and lifted them from the water. The big hook-jawed male trout lay quietly in my hands, even though its bright pattern of spots, its glistening sides, were exposed to the air. I held it up so that everyone on the bank, some of them open-mouthed, could see.

"You're right," I said. "It's not a fourteen incher. More like eighteen, at least." Then I lowered it into the stream, tipped my hands, and watched it laze back under the sheltering stone.

Though he didn't talk about it, Grampa Jesse was Abenaki Indian. He never said that anything he taught me when I was a child had to do with his heritage. It was for me to figure out later in life when I would try to raise my own children the way he and Grama Bowman had brought me up—never hitting me, giving me the freedom of the woods and the streams, and showing me more by example than by telling me what to do and what not to do. So it was that Grampa Jesse taught me how to tickle a trout.

I was in sixth grade. Aside from getting high grades and being the first one with the answers, I wasn't doing that well. I was one of the smallest kids in my class. I had glasses. I was from the outlying countryside beyond the town of Saratoga Springs and thus, by definition, a "hick." Far from "cool," a new term just creeping into our vocabularies. I also read too many books, was not good at sports, and told my teacher whenever anyone picked on me. Thus I was a brain, a nerd, and a squealer all in one neat package. I felt like I was cursed.

When that summer came, fishing season came with it. It both excited and worried me. My Dad, with whom I spent very little time, was a taxidermist and an outdoorsman of the first rank. When he went fishing he always caught his limit, and when he hunted, he always got his deer. Sooner or later, I knew, he would tell my grandparents that he wanted to take me trout fishing. Sure enough, on a glorious day in late June, he did just that. As always, my sister Mary Ann went along. Dad had brought three spinning rods to fish with. One was his own, one was Mary Ann's, and one was for me to use. At the lake, Mary Ann was the first to cast her spinner into the water from the dock. After years of practice, she was an ace with a spinning rod. She caught a trout on her first cast. I tried throwing out my line, the unfamiliar rod as awkward as a club in my hand. The line whirred and tangled. A backlash. My father said something under his breath and grabbed the pole from me.

"I'll cast it for you. You can just reel it in. You can do that, can't you?"

I nodded. If I'd tried to say anything I would have burst into tears.

When I got home late that afternoon, dropped off in front of my grandparents' general store by my father, who drove off before I reached the front door, I handed Grama a string of ten fat brook trout.

"You did so well, Sonny," she said.

"No, I didn't." I said. "I only caught one little trout and Dad said it was too small. Mary Ann caught all these."

And then I started to cry. I buried my head against my grandmother's shoulder and sobbed and wished I'd never been born. Why was it that I couldn't ever do anything right?

My grandfather's leathery hand was patting my shoulder, but he didn't say anything then or at dinner. He waited until the next morning.

"Come on," he said. We climbed into the old square blue Plymouth and drove up 9N, turned onto Porter Corners Road, then up the mountain where he parked the car near the South Branch. Then and there, he showed me how to tickle a trout, how to coax it into your hands and lift it out of the water. It wasn't easy and I was soon soaking wet, but I kept trying until I finally succeeded, until a seven inch brook trout was gently moving in my hands.

"What do I do now?" I said.

"Did you ask it to trust ye?" Grampa said.

I nodded. Grampa nodded back. I carefully lowered my hands and let the trout go.

It was an unusually hot dry summer that year. By late August, Bell Brook, the little stream behind my grandparents' old house, was going dry in places, leaving trout stranded in shrinking pools. I walked the creek with a bucket, rescuing trout to carry them further upstream where the stream still flowed.

In the years that have passed since that day in June, I've caught many trout that way, always returning them to the water again. I've grown to be tall and strong, to be an athlete, to have friends, to raise children of my own. But that little boy who couldn't catch a fish with a pole is still there inside of me. And he smiles as I am smiling now at the thought of how much began with that gift of trust my grandfather gave me when he taught me how to tickle a trout.

HOLLYHOCKS

Hollyhocks. My grandmother's garden was edged with hollyhocks. Maybe you've seen them, an old fashioned plant that shoots a stalk up from the fan of wide green leaves at its base. When I was little I thought hollyhock stalks were as tall as the maple trees. They were only the height of a tall man, but when you're only knee-high yourself, that is plenty tall. Knee-high, that is how my Grampa described me sometimes. Knee-high to a gopher, to be more precise. I was a really little kid. All through grade school and even into high school I was the shrimp with glasses.

"You'll grow." That is what Grama told me. I wanted to believe her, but it stretched the imagination. Especially when I came home from second grade with my glasses broken again or a new bruise from one of the bullies who saw me as easy pickings. I was only slightly more able to defend myself than road-kill, way low on the schoolyard foodchain.

Do you know what the foodchain is? Even by second grade I was reading a lot about nature, books by such naturalists as William Beebe and John Muir and Edwin Way Teale and Roger Tory Peterson. So I knew the foodchain. Big fish eat little fish and little fish eat littler fish and so on. What kind of fish was I? I wasn't. I was plankton.

My grandmother was usually the first to console me when I came home as bedraggled as a butterfly that had been caught in a whirlwind.

"One day," she'd say as she drove me yet again to Dr. Boyle, the optometrist who would make up yet another set of eyeglasses for me, "you're going to be bigger than those boys who picked on you. Then they're all going to want to be your friends."

Do I even have to say that I didn't believe her one bit? Plankton is plankton.

But there were those hollyhocks. In late summer the flowers spiralled from the top third of the tall spike that rose toward the sun like a church spire, or maybe the Washington Monument. Those flowers looked like the hibiscus blossoms I'd seen in a movie about the south seas. And the lilac spikes came in all colors. Some were as white as the cream on top of the glass milk bottles. Some were the moist red of the lips of those women in the ads in *Life* magazine. Some were as dark purple as the fabric of the night sky when there were no stars. Pink, yellow, just about every shade of the rainbow. The blossoms were a little sticky to the touch, their petals glossed yellow by the pollen from the stamens. Lots of pollen. The rubythroated hummingbirds loved the hollyhocks for their nectar and for the little insects they could pluck from the flowers. They practically tore them apart as they whizzed from one blossom to the next. You could almost hear those little whirring feathered rockets saying "Ohboyohboyohboy!" to themselves when they came upon a garden graced by a generous forest of hollyhocks.

One summer day, as I stood among the hollyhocks, getting a stiff neck from peering up at them, my grandfather reached out and plucked off a dead blossom. I hadn't even heard him come up behind me. He could move like that, making less noise than the wind through the leaves. He went down on one knee, which took him a little effort to do. Strong as he was from shoveling coal at the butter plant, his joints were stiff by late in the day and it was almost evening.

"Lookit this, Sonny," he said. At the base of that wilted blossom was a ball of green. He broke it open and spread out the circle of little seeds, flat as tiny pale coins.

I knew all about seeds. I'd read about the fertlization between pistil and stamen in the flower, how bees and birds carried pollen from one plant to another, how the flower withered and left the seeds behind. But, I hadn't really thought about it. It was book knowledge. I was always big on that. Grampa, who could barely read, respected that kind of knowing, but had another sort of wisdom that came from the doing of things, from touching the earth.

He carefully worked one seed free and placed it in my outstretched palm. Then he looked up at the hollyhocks, that were like giant redwoods over both our heads.

"Lookit that," he said.

I looked and I saw. He didn't have to say anything else. The little seed could turn into that tower of blossoms. It would just take a few seasons for it to happen. The knowing of this touched my heart.

Among our old Algonquin people there is a belief in the *dodem*, an understanding that there are other beings in the world wiser than humans. These beings are connected to our lives and our spirits and act as teachers and protectors. Those who are into the spiritual edge of native cultures talk a lot these days about totem animals. They even sell decks of cards with impressive creatures like the bear and the eagle and the wolf on them. Non-Indians get all excited about dramatic totem animals like those. Everybody seems to want to identify with some kind of big predator.

That day, though, when I was in the second grade and standing small in my grandmother's garden, my grandfather gave me one of my dodems. And though I stand more than six feet tall as a man, those sweet giving flowers still tower over me in my dreams. Hollyhocks.

ACKNOWLEDGEMENTS

I'd like to express my thanks to the following publications where earlier versions of these stories first appeared:

"At the End of Ridge Road"—*The Colors of Nature,* edited by Alison H. Deming and Lauret E. Savoy, Milkweed Editions, 2002.

"Bone Girl"—*Earth Song, Sky Spirit,* edited by Clifford E. Trafzer, Doubleday, 1992.

"Bad Meat," "Bearskin Robe," "Sojy Visits His Friends"—*Without Reservation*, edited by Kateri Akiwenzie-Damm, Kegedonce Press, 2003.

"The Hungry One"—*Skins*, Edited by Kateri Akiwenzie-Damm and Josie Douglas, Kegedonce Press, 2000.

"The Snapping Turtle"—*When I Was Your Age*, Volume Two, edited by Amy Ehrlich, Candlewick Press, 1999.

"Sounds of Thunder"—*Shattered, Stories of Childood and War*, edited by Jennifer Armstrong, Knopf, 2002

"Tickling a Trout"—*25 Read Aloud Stories for Teaching Powerful Writing*, edited by Bob Sizoo, Scholastic, 2001.

ABOUT THE AUTHOR

Joseph Bruchac lives with his wife Carol in Greenfield Center, New York. He is the author of over 100 volumes of poetry, fiction, memoir, children's stories and anthology collections. His most recent novel is *Whisper in the Dark* (HarperCollins, 2005).

ABOUT THE ARTIST

Chris Charlebois is an Abenaki artist and flute player who lives in New Hampshire. He has been showing his work and performing since he was a teenager. In 2003, he performed coast to coast to promote his first album, "Kisses From a Blind Child." He has created illustrations for many publications.